The Last Scout

OTHER SAGEBRUSH LARGE PRINT WESTERNS BY
WILL COOK

Apache Ambush

The Last Scout

WILL COOK

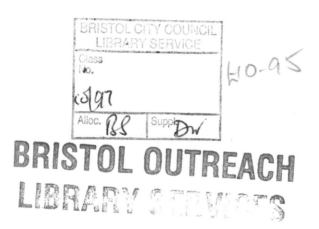

Sagebrush
Large Print Westerns

Library of Congress Cataloging in Publication Data

Cook, Will.
  The last scout / Will Cooks.
    p.   cm.
  ISBN 1-57490-055-2 (alk. paper)
  1. Large type books. I. Title.
  [PS3553.O5547L37   1997]
  813'.54--dc21   97-17585
                                                   CIP

Cataloguing in Publication Data is available from
the British Library and the National Library of Australia.

Cataloguing in Publication Data is available from
the British Library and the National Library of Australia.

Sagebrush Large Print Westerns are published in the United States
and Canada by Thomas T. Beeler, Publisher, Box 659, Hampton
Falls, New Hampshire 03844-0659. ISBN 1-57490-055-2

Published in the United Kingdom, Eire, and the Republic of South
Africa by Isis Publishing Ltd, 7 Centremead, Osney Mead, Oxford
OX2 0ES England. ISBN 0-7531-5592-3

Published in Australia and New Zealand by Australian Large Print
Audio & Video Pty Ltd, 17 Mohr Street, Tullamarine, Victoria, 3043,
Australia. ISBN 1-86340-735-9

Manufactured in the United States of America

CHAPTER 1

I NEVER SAW MY GRANDFATHER UNTIL I WAS seventeen years old, but I had always known that he was famous. My mother had said so, and she named me after him, Page; that was her maiden name before she married father.

And grandfather was the one they called Wind-River Page, and he got that name in the days of William Bent and the great fur trade, and just knowing that he was coming to live with us filled me with excitement. I got out of bed a little earlier than usual to make sure that my brothers, Ralph and Joe, got off to school on time, then drove dad to the mine; he was general superintendent and they were getting ready to break through to the richest vein Deadwood had ever seen.

When I got home, mother said, "Sit down and eat your breakfast, Page. I swear, if anything more happens today, I'll go mad." She put food on the table and flounced around the kitchen and watching her, I couldn't help 'but think how high strung she was and how much she enjoyed being like that. At forty-five she was still tall and slender and her hair was as dark as the underside of a stove lid. She had Indian blood in her all right, Cheyenne, I think; she was the youngest daughter of one of grandfather's eight wives. You'd think that that alone would sort of cast her into lifelong disgrace, but it didn't. That was a difficult thing to understand about people, how they'd gossip because some town girl married a soldier, as though she'd ruined her life or something, and then think it was wonderful because you had some Indian blood, like you'd overcome some strong handicap.

1

I guess there'd been some talk about my father twenty years ago. He'd been a soldier then, a sergeant, and the way he tells it, he was at the camp store one day when Wind-River Page came on the post with mother. She'd been dressed in Indian getup and all, and father just took one look and knew he'd been had. I suppose they all said he ruined his career. Didn't turn out that way though.

"Page, will you please eat and stop mooning?"

Her voice kind of snapped me awake; I finished breakfast and went out in back of the house to hitch up the buggy. I could hear mother in the house, rattling dishes; it was a sure sign that she was agitated, and of late I'd begun to wonder whether she wanted grandfather to come and live with us or not.

She wasn't an easy woman to figure out, and father made no claim to having done it.

When the mare was hitched, I went back into the house. She'd finished the dishes and had filled a scrub bucket with soapy water. "Ma," I said, "It's almost eight! The stage is going to be here."

"You go," she said. "I've got more than I can do here as is."

I looked at her for a minute. "Ma, don't you want to meet the stage?"

She never did like those questions that stuck her, so she made a casual face and shrugged. "I don't see no need for the whole family to make such a fuss. Page, you're getting to be a manly part of the Sheridans. You meet the stage while I tidy up the place."

"You scrubbed it from top to bottom yesterday," I pointed out.

"Now don't tell me how to conduct my affairs," she snapped. "Go on or you'll be late."

2

I went out and got in the buggy and drove through the narrow rutted streets to the center of town. Deadwood, in the early seventies, was just something that had been slapped together with no thought of making it permanent. The hills were full of minerals and covered with a blanket of timber and sawmills sprang up on every street corner. This was all hilly country and no one bothered to level the lots before putting up buildings. On one side of the main street there would be a dozen steps leading to the porch level, while on the other, the doors were right down on the ground and during the rains, all the loose top soil oozed in until it sometimes stood ankle deep in the stores.

Deadwood was a busy, bustling town, with its share of good things and bad. We had our notorious ones and they walked around all day long with big pistols on their hips, and played cards half the night, and now and then they'd shoot somebody and everyone would talk about it for a week. Then we had a few like Bill Hickok that people left strictly alone; I noticed that even the toughs tipped their hats to him and took care not to brush against him when he was sitting or walking around.

I managed to drive the buggy through the dense traffic and parked near the express office. There was no sense in getting down; a man would just get embroiled in the pedestrian traffic, and besides, I could see more from the buggy seat.

Marshal Jim Bell came across the street, shouldering his way through moving horsemen. He stopped by the off wheel and smiled. "You stuck here or just waitin'?"

"Waiting," I said. "My grandfather's coming in on the stage today."

Bell's smile widened. "Your mother's side or your father's?"

3

"Ma's."

"Good, then I won't have to go through my files and see if he's wanted for horse stealin'." He was a big, broad-shouldered man in his young thirties, rather flat of face, but pleasant mannered, and I knew of a few men who had mistaken that for softness. Bell had a reputation around Deadwood, and other parts of the country I guess. He wasn't a shooting man, although he could if it came to that. But he wasn't a gunman. I knew Jim Bell well; he came to our house often enough, and he always struck me as a man who preferred peace above all else. "Your dad go up to the mine this morning?"

"I guess they're close to a new vein," I said.

Jim Bell's smiled broadened. "Page, let me tell you something about mining men and miners. They're always near a new vein, or about to strike it rich, or something." He shook his head in sympathy. "Well, I hope they do hit it. With all the robberies they've been havin' this last year, it's bein' stolen faster than they can dig it out and smelt it down." He reached up and slapped me on the thigh. "See you around, Page."

He worked through the crowd and on down the street, and I settled down to wait for the stage. It was hard for me to imagine what my grandfather would be like. He'd be old, of course. Father had made some mention of seventy, so I was all prepared to help him down off the stage and avoid the ruts going home.

The stage was a little late, which wasn't unusual. The street traffic scattered to the edge of the walk and the stage came to a sliding halt before the express office. Hank Bowers was handling the ribbons and he wrapped them around the brake handle before getting down. Beside him on the high seat sat another man, a very old

4

man in a dust-powdered dark suit. As soon as Bowers got down, this man dropped to the ground, scorning the wheel as a step.

This couldn't be grandfather!

The passengers were getting down; they moved quickly as though they were glad the ride was over. There was a woman who rushed into the waiting arms of a man, and two fellas who worked for Big-Deal Collins, and a third man, another heavy with guns and a sour expression on his face.

I guess it was grandfather all right.

He got his luggage from the boot and looked around. When he saw me, he gave me a study for a moment, then came over, his short legs giving him a rolling gait, like a seaman a long time away from shore.

"Be you a Sheridan?" he asked. His face was a mask of lines, a matrix of age and hard living. He wore a dense mustache, and his eyebrows were thickets, shadowing his eyes, giving him a fierce look. "Of course you be. You got the eyes."

And before I could say anything, he reached up, fisted a handful of my coat and hauled me flying from the buggy seat. I struck the dust of the street and rolled against the forelegs of a horse. The animal shied and the rider hurriedly pulled him up. The crowd suddenly stopped to see what was going on.

Stunned, I looked at the old man and asked, "What did you do that for?"

"I want to see what kind of a man you be," he said. "Wrestle me, boy. Put me down and then I'll know."

"I—I don't want to fight you, grandpa," I said. "You're —old."

It made him laugh and he clapped his hands flat against his lean stomach and let out a ringing whoop.

"This be a fun fight, boy. On your feet like a man."

Someone in the crowd said, "Go on and lick him, kid. Make him happy."

It seemed like a funny thing to say, but I got up, not because I wanted to wrestle, but because I didn't like sitting on the ground, especially after somebody put me there.

"Grandpa, can't we just shake hands and go home?"

"I'll shake," he said and took my hand. But he only gave it one pump and then wheeled and kited me over his shoulder. That ground seemed a lot harder the second time and I grunted loudly. The crowd laughed and some wag made a smart remark.

"Watch him, kid. I don't think he likes you."

When I got up the second time, I was through fooling around, grandfather or not. I grappled with him and found his strength not only equal to mine, but more determined. We swayed like two trees with branches entwined, and there was no getting an advantage on him.

I managed to throw him down; actually I just tripped him, and he hit and seemed to bounce to his feet. Just about the time we were set to go at it again, Jim Bell came through the crowd and stiff armed both of us.

"When the hell's goin' on here?" he asked.

"Friendly doin's between kin," Wind-River Page snapped. I could see that he hated interference from anyone, including the law.

"Page," Bell said softly, "why don't you take this old coot home?"

"What the hell do you think I've been trying to do?" I stepped over and put grandfather's luggage in the buggy, then got in. He stood there a moment, looking at Jim Bell, then he got into the rig and I clucked the horse into motion. As we drove away, I said, "A fine thing. The whole town'll be talking about it."

"There's worse to talk about," grandfather said. He looked at me and grinned. "You're a strong boy. Need a mite of toughenin' up, but you're a strong boy."

He exasperated me and I let it show." Grandpa, you made a fool of yourself."

"You ain't sore about that," he said. "You're sore 'cause you think I made a fool of you."

His point was beyond argument, so I said nothing more. When we got home, I stopped in front of the house and got down, meaning to take his luggage. But he was of an independent mind and carried it himself.

Mother must have been looking out, waiting, because she opened the door just as we stepped on the porch. Grandpa stopped and looked at her, and she looked at him, then burst into tears.

Grandpa said, "Time ain't changed you much, Dawn."

Then we all went into the house and mother made him sit in the best chair and fussed over him until he waved her away. I'd never seen her face like this, as though she were trying to make up all at once for something she'd done over a period of time.

She brought in some coffee and seemed to have calmed down. "I've fixed you a room upstairs," she said. "You can stay as long as you like."

"That's kind of you, Dawn," he said. Then he leaned back and looked around. We didn't have the best house in town, but pretty near. He looked at the furniture and the rugs and the pictures on the walls and I just couldn't tell whether he approved of any of it or not.

He wasn't an easy man to figure, even when he wanted you to understand him.

7

"Got three boys, huh?"

Mother nodded. "Ralph and Joe are in school."

Grandpa nodded. "Well, I never could see the advantage to readin' and writin', but I guess it's all right for those that can afford it."

I noticed that mother kept looking at me, and then I glanced down at my pants and saw the dust on them. So I got up and said, "I guess I'll ride out to the mine."

She probably had an objection to this, but I got out of the house before she could voice it. I put the buggy away and turned the horse into the stall, then saddled my own mare. Later she'd probably have a word or two to say to me about dashing off like that, but I didn't care. Maybe it was just that I was reaching the age where I had to obey the dictates of my own mind, and not someone else's.

Leaving town, I took one of the hill roads; there were dozens, some no more than faint trails leading to a man's diggings. The hills were full of miners, all boring into the face of the land, all working their backs aching for gold. And the gold was there. Hardly a month passed when someone didn't make some kind of a strike.

The Big Dutchman was the biggest mine, and my father ran it. They owned the crusher and the smelter, and not only worked their own ore, but that of nearly every miner around. It was all on a percentage, but it paid, since it was cheaper to haul bullion than ore.

Well, it would have been cheaper if the danged robbers weren't so well organized. The Big Dutchman alone had lost eighty thousand dollars in the last four months to the robbers. And the independent miners had probably lost half that.

And so far, no posse had been able to catch up with the bandits.

Someone had once joked that it was better business than mining, only it wasn't a joke any more.

The main mine offices were anchored against a steep hillside, and I tied my horse and walked up the long eight of steps to father's office. The door of his office was open, I saw, so I knocked and went in. He was digging through some filing cabinets and turned his head toward me, then motioned for me to sit down until he was through.

He found the papers he wanted and took them to his desk, then sat down. "Grandpa get here all right?"

"Yes, sir, but he wasn't what I expected."

"What did you expect?"

I shrugged. "I don't know. Maybe something like some of the old-timers around Deadwood."

"Grandpa's been civilized," father said.

"He has?" I was surprised to hear this. Then I told him about the wrestling match, and he laughed heartily over it.

"I fought him once, just before your mother and I were married. Didn't lick him though. However, he must have thought I put up a good scrap because he let us get married."

"Pa, where's grandpa been living all these years?" He looked at me rather sharply, as though he wished I hadn't asked that. But I was determined to find out. "I mean, you and ma never talked about him much, except these last few months. Now he's come to live with us."

Father stripped the wrapper off a cigar and put a match to it. When he got it drawing good, he said, "Close the door." I did and came back and sat down. "This is going to take some understanding on your part, Page. What I mean is, we're not perfect. We make mistakes and we're sorry for them later. Some of them

9

we can't correct, and for those we must be forgiven. Your mother's never been too happy about her Indian blood. When she was four, she left the tribe and went to live with white people. She was raised white, went to school, got a good education. Then one day her father came and took her back to the blanket. Five years of that, until I married her." He drew deeply on his cigar. "I've always refused to believe that she hated him for it. Rather I like to think that she resented it deeply."

"She cried when she saw him," I said.

He nodded. "Yes, and I think she was crying for herself rather than for him. But it's something that'll have to work out, Page. We've got to give it time."

"What's grandpa been doing all this time?"

Father's face settled into serious lines. "He's been taking life easy, son. For many years he worked for the army, as a scout. Eight years ago they put him out to pasture. He's had his last scout." He looked at me, as he often did when he gave me half an answer and hoped I'd be satisfied with it. But I wasn't and he knew it. "He's been in an old soldier's home, Page. Your mother signed the papers because we thought it was best at the time."

"Gosh," I said. "That's awful! Why, it must have been like jail."

"It might have been just that bad, to him," father said. "But we're going to change all that, Page. We're going to try."

"Yes, sir. That's good, because I like him." I got up and turned to the door. "Could I borrow your shotgun? I kind of got the idea I'd go out and get a brace of birds for supper. You know, just to celebrate. I guess he's got a taste for wild game, huh, pa?"

Father smiled at me. "I think it's a good gesture. The

10

gun's in the closet there. Some shells on the top shelf."

I got the gun and dropped six or eight shells in my coat pocket, then went out and mounted my horse. Bird hunting was one of my favorite pastimes and I knew where they were thickest, even though it was an hour's ride away. Three or four fat hens in the pot and served over mother's dumplings would make grandpa feel at home, and I wanted him to feel that way right off. Perhaps it was because young people are insecure to begin with, not knowing their true place in the world, that they are sensitive to the insecurity of others. I could imagine how grandpa felt, and how hard he tried to cover it. He'd been out of touch for years and it would take some doing to get back. And some understanding on everyone's part.

My hunting ground wasn't private, but there weren't many men around Deadwood who liked to hunt birds, so I could usually count on having it to myself. But not that day. I'd hardly dismounted when I heard the bellow of a ten gauge Greener, then the excited bark of Dale Buckley's hound dog. He was across the hollow, and I homed on the dog's bark and started toward him. Twenty minutes later I entered a clearing and found Buckley sitting beneath a tree, pipe clenched in his jaws, a brace of birds by his side. The dog ran to greet me and jumped up and planted his enormous paws on my chest so he could lick my face.

Buckley smiled and took the pipe from his mouth "Just the man I want to see, Page. I need a good shotgunner. Missed three shots already."

"If you want to work together," I said, "I'll split the bag with you."

"You always say the right thing," Buckley said and invited me to sit down.

11

He was a man of twenty-seven or eight, an Eastern man, with manners, and high courage and a sharp mind, and I liked him. I didn't know much about his background except that his father was important and he'd sent his son west to learn the express business from the ground up. And I guess everyone would agree that Dale Buckley was the best division manager the company had ever had. He plugged all those little leaks in operation that cost money, and even made passenger fares pay.

But he couldn't do anything about the holdups, and he tried.

We hunted birds and talked and he said that his sister was coming out for the summer, and he didn't sound too happy about it. He claimed she was lovely, and I cut that estimate down to "pretty," right away, and promised I'd take her around a bit, as a favor. We talked about all the robberies and Buckley said he was going to put on some more men, which made sense to me. Any robber with a lick of sense would shy clear of a well-armed coach with an alert shotgun guard.

I'd done some hunting with Dale Buckley before, and somehow, he could just never get the hang of a shotgun. Maybe it wasn't his weapon; I've since discovered that some men just take naturally to a certain kind of gun. "You take Bill Hickok for example. Why, he could get those long-barreled .44s into action so fast you wouldn't believe it. A couple of times I tried a draw with dad's Army .44 and I swear if it had been loaded, I'd have shot my leg off.

But a shotgun felt good to me, and every time we rushed a bird, I'd whip it up and fire both barrels before Dale Buckley could even get set. We downed nine birds, or I downed them, with nine shots; I had to borrow some shells from Dale before the afternoon wore out.

We split the bag, and rode back to town together. He said, "Page, you're a damned whiz with a shotgun. I'd swear that two of those shots were at seventy yards. And they were clean kills too."

"It's a talent," I said, bragging a little, but kidding too.

"Well, talent or not, I hate to see it go to waste." He stopped his horse and dismounted, then unbuckled his saddle bag. "I've got some buckshot loads here. Will you do a little shooting for me?"

"Sure," I said and tied up the horse.

We were in a small swale, with hills on both sides, and Buckley gave me the shells before walking out sixty or seventy yards. I couldn't figure out what he had in mind, but I was willing to go along with it. He gathered up some clods of dirt, then said, "I'll throw, and you bust as many as you can."

That was pretty simple business, until he started heaving them every which way, high and low, and I had to really buckle down. I was breaking nine out of ten; then he stopped throwing.

"All right, now turn your back to me. When I yell, you turn because I'll have thrown."

It was silly, but fun, a real challenge to eye and arm, and I broke six in a row that way. I'd never seen Dale Buckley so happy.

"Page, will you sit down on that rock over there? That's fine. Now lean the shotgun against you. Keep your hands on it though. When I throw, shoot. No, don't look at me! I'll yell."

This turned out to be tough shooting, for he sailed them left and right and a few in front of me that I didn't expect, but I guess I broke twelve out of sixteen. He was tiring and my shoulder was beginning to ache and he walked over to where I sat.

"Have you had your fun?" I asked.

"I've had a real education," Dale Buckley said. "Page, how would you like to work for me, a hundred a month?"

"Huh?"

He laughed softly. "Let's say that the rock you're sitting on is the seat of a stage and those clods I've thrown a holdup man's head. I like the odds on you being able to hit where others miss."

The thought of shooting anyone sobered me considerably. "Now wait a minute. I'd be no good as a shotgun guard."

"Name me a better man."

That was a hell of a way to put a thing; what did he expect me to say? I just shook my head. "Your theory is cock-eyed. A rock is steady, but a stage is moving, bobbing around. Naw, I couldn't cut it."

"You're not scared, are you?"

I bristled a little. "Let's not be funny, huh?"

He laughed and thumped me on the shoulder. "All right, I've got something else, if you're game."

"Talk."

"I'll ride on ahead and have a stage hitched up. Then I'll go on down the road apiece and hang up eight or ten small bags of flour. You come on in and wait for me at the express office. You can sit by the driver and he'll hit his pace. Keep your eyes peeled and whenever you see one of those flour bags, cut loose."

"That sounds like fun," I said. "All right, but I won't guarantee a thing."

"Sold," Buckley said and stepped into the saddle. He rode away, not wasting any time, and I mounted

14

leisurely. The whole notion was kind of foolish, me going to work as a shotgun guard. Not that I was against work, but I'd hoped to get on at the bank in the fall; it seemed more in my line. And besides, I was only seventeen, and one ought to be a full man before accepting such responsibility.

But I knew Dale Buckley; he had an argument for everything, and usually a good one. He'd bring up Wyatt Earp, and how he'd handled the same kind of a job at fifteen and made a reputation for himself.

You really couldn't win with Dale Buckley.

I dropped the birds off at home, then went to the express office. The stage was waiting, the driver talking to Bill Hickok and Marshal Jim Bell. When I dismounted, Bell said, "Gabe tells me you're going to do a little shooting."

"Aw, it's just something Dale cooked up," I said.

Hickok said, "You don't mind if we go along, do you?"

He'd never spoken to me before and it gave me an odd feeling. "No, I don't care."

Dale Buckley came back to town and flung off by the hitch rail. "I've put up flour bags for about a mile and a half, Page." He gave me a clap on the back and motioned for me to get on the high seat with the driver. Buckley and the others got into the coach and he closed the door. "Let her go, Gabe!"

A stage seat is a precarious perch, I discovered, and the only way I could gain security was to hook my toes under the rod running across the front of the box. We rattled out of town at a clip designed to cut minutes from an existing record, and all the time I sat there loose-hipped, bobbing to the pitch and roll.

The first bag came as a surprise; it was tied waist high

15

in a bush and I darned near missed seeing it. I shot and was rewarded with a burst of white flour, then only had time to wheel around and blast the other one on the other side of the road. Gabe drove like a man gone mad, unmindful of the shotgun roaring about his ears; a miscue on my part and I'd have blown his head off.

I reloaded and just in time, for I saw two bags hanging not three feet apart. It was one of those classic duck shots, about fifty yards, and just the right spread apart to get both with a shot between them. I knew that I scored because Dale let out a war whoop, and the stage thundered on.

Out of the eight bags he'd hung, I scattered seven, and when Bill Hickok inspected the one I missed, he found a neat .32 caliber hole in it. Just one buck shot, but enough to make a man sick.

We stopped along the road and Jim Bell stood there, smiling. "Page, that's the best shotgun work I've ever seen. How about it, Bill?"

"I wouldn't want a quarrel with you," he said. "It's good shootin' in any man's book, young fella." He glanced at Dale Buckley. "I take it you had something in mind here besides amusement."

"Sure did," Buckley said. "Well, Page, what about it?"

"I feel like the guy who braided the rope that hung him," I said. Then I looked up at Gabe, his jaws methodically working on a cud of tobacco. "Did I make you nervous? The shooting got a little wild there."

"Sonny, with you on the box there, I'd feel real good."

Jim Bell laughed. "Wait a minute! Dale, are you hiring him?"

"If he'll take it," Buckley said. "A hundred a month,

16

Page, and only the gold runs."

"That's as much as you make, Bell," Hickok said.

I never did know what swayed me. Maybe it was because I was a kid standing among men, good men, and having their genuine respect. Anyway, I offered Dale Buckley my hand on it.

"When do I start?"

"Tomorrow night. The Big Dutchman is shipping."

"You ought to keep that a secret," Bell said sternly.

Buckley shook his head. "No, if anyone's fool enough to try a holdup now, then I want them to learn their lesson in a hurry. Come on, let's go back to town. I'll have to bond you, Page, and there's an application blank for you to fill out."

By the time these details were attended to, it was near six and I had to get home for supper. As I hurried along it struck me as being funny, my taking a big job on one hand, then hurrying because I didn't want my mother to bawl me out.

Dad was home, and my two brothers; they were little pests, always ragging me for this and that. Ralph was eleven, and it took about six nickels a week to buy him off. Joe was nine and hadn't wised up yet as to how much a big brother was good for.

Grandpa was sitting in the living room while mother set the table, and he looked like he wasn't sure whether he should keep out of her way or help. I guess that is a problem with older people. Dad was doing his best to strike up a conversation, but it wasn't easy. A lot of years lay between them, and all grandpa knew about were the old days, and dad wasn't interested in going over them.

Eating gave us something to do together, and I waited until the meal was well along before making my

17

announcement. I had a notion that it was going to be unpopular.

"Dad, I got a job this afternoon."

"Oh?" He went on eating, and now and then picked a piece of shot out of the meat.

"What kind of a job?" mother asked. I glanced at her; she was passing the gravy to grandpa, and in her own mind she had already put down a few likely selections, like clerking in the store, or helping in the assay office.

"I'm riding shotgun for Dale Buckley," I said.

Best to get it out and get it over with. Father looked at me as though to warn me that his day had been difficult and not to start joking. Mother just stared; she knew I wasn't joking at all.

She said, "That's ridiculous."

"What's ridiculous about it? I'm a whiz with a shotgun."

"A coward's weapon," Grandpa said.

"You keep out of this," mother warned. "Page Sheridan, after supper you march right uptown and tell Dale Buckley that you're not riding shotgun."

"I'm sorry," I said. "I can't do that. I gave my word."

"If you give it, stick to it," grandfather said.

Father said, "This is family business, if you please."'

That's right," grandpa said, "Remind me that I ain't family." He got up from the table and stomped into the living room.

Ralph laughed. "Now see what you've done, Page?"

"Oh, dry up!" I snapped. There was no arguing with mother, so I didn't even try, I turned to my father, to appeal to his manly sense of pride and his judgment. "Dad, I can handle the job. I took it and I'm going to keep it. It pays a hundred a month."

"And a free coffin?" He wiped a hand across his

18

mouth, then fingered his mustache. "Page, I always thought you had good sense. Obviously I was wrong. When does this idiotic employment begin?"

"Tomorrow night," I said. "I'm going with the gold shipment."

Their appetites vanished, and I felt like the devil for causing it all. Father said, "Well, you're nearly a man, and I suppose this had to happen sooner or later." He sighed as though very weary. "They say a young man's first jump is usually his biggest. Let's hope you pull out before it's your last."

When he got up, mother said, "Fred, is that all you've got to say?"

He shrugged. "Look at his face. He looks like a bulldog locked onto a bone. You can't talk to him, Dawn. He'll go his own way whether we like it or not."

Then he threw down his napkin and went into the parlor.

CHAPTER 2

DALE BUCKLEY TOLD ME TO BE AT THE EXPRESS OFFICE AT six, so as soon as I ate supper, I went to my room to change clothes. For serious hunting I had a heavy pair of duck pants and an old brush jacket; I figured these would do fine and was buttoning up when father came in.

"I'd like to give you a lot of advice," he said. "Like, keep your eyes open, and don't go, and a lot of other contradictory things. But you're going to do what you want, so I'll say no more. However, I want you to know that it isn't easy."

"Sure, pa. I'll bet your father said the same thing."

He smiled and thumped me on the shoulder. "See you in two days, huh?"

I nodded and went out of the house quickly, not bothering to say goodbye to anyone else. Grandpa was sitting on the porch and he got up and walked with me to the express office. For a spell there he didn't say anything, then he said, "A young fellas first step into a man's world is a big one. But I wouldn't worry none about anybody but myself from now on."

"What do you mean?"

"Well, a fella will get to thinkin' about how he's made his ma cry, and his pa mad, and he'll put his mind on it instead of his business. Could get yourself killed that way."

"You've got a point, grandpa," I said.

"Another thing too," he said. "A man picks his work because he is what he is. When a man ain't afraid to try himself, to find out what he is, he'll take a job with some risk to it. When he ain't man enough to do that, he clerks in a store, or counts plews another man fetches to him. It's always been that way, boy. Back in the days of the fur trade, them rich titled fellas would come out and run the tradin' posts. They'd faunch about in knee britches and sniff snuff and keep books. Then they'd go back to New Orleans and tell what a tough time it was, how cold it got in the winter." He laughed "They thought they was livin', boy, but the livin' was a far piece out, to a place they'd never see, on account of it took a man to just get there. You see them far places, boy. You go when the itch gets you, and don't come back 'til you've seen it all."

We stopped in front of the express office. "You're an old pirate, grandpa."

He took it the way I meant it, as a compliment, and he

gave me a near toothless grin. "Yeah, I've bayed at the moon and made a couple of trips to hell just to see what it was like down there. But I got no regrets. Life's a strong taste, boy, and only a few are man enough not to choke on the sweetness of it, or retch on the gall."

I left him and went inside to Dale Buckley's office. He was eating his supper at his desk, and he waved me into a chair. "Present for you," he said and nodded toward the corner. I walked over and picked up a brand new shotgun, a ten gauge double with thirty inch barrels, a magnificently balanced weapon. On the back of a nearby chair, a bandoleer of brass cased shells hung, and I buckled this around my waist.

"Like it?" Buckley asked. "My father gave that to me last year. Imported from England. The left barrel has what they call a choke. I don't really understand it, but I've been told that the last six inches of bore is squeezed down slightly. It keeps the shot in a more compact group, raising the effective range to a hundred yards. Anyway, I killed a mule deer with it last fall at that range."

"I may try it out a couple of times on the way to Rapid City," I said.

Buckley smiled. "I expected it to be used." Then he let his expression grow serious. "Page, if you have to point that at a man, don't hesitate to shoot."

"If he has a mask over his face and a gun in his hand," I said, "I won't." I took out my pocket watch and looked at it. "I'm a little early."

"We're going to have a meeting before you leave," Buckley said. "Now let me finish my supper."

I sat down and examined the shotgun, then Jim Bell came in, grinned at me and slid a chair around so that he could tip it against the wall. Buckley finished his pie

21

and coffee and pushed the tray aside, then looked at the wall clock. A man's familiar footstep sounded in the outer office, then father came in.

Buckley said, "Close the door and lock it, Fred." When this was done, father sat down. "I guess we can bring the meeting to order," Buckley said, smiling. "It's my opinion that everyone in town knows we're sending out a gold shipment tonight. Have you heard any talk, Jim?"

Bell shrugged. "The usual. Bets are being taken, five to seven, that it's held up."

"That's a pleasant thought," father said glumly.

"We have to assume that all shipments are going to be held up," Dale Buckley said solemnly.

"Yes," father said, "and if the score so far means anything, we've got to assume that the robbers know as much about our shipping plans as we do." He looked at all of us. "We've got to plug the leak, gentlemen."

"Find it first," Jim Bell said. "When you stop to think of how many know about the gold shipments, it's no wonder we're held up." He added them up on his fingers. "The gold has to be loaded; how many men do you use, Fred? Six? Eight?"

"Six usually, but they can be trusted."

"No one can be trusted," Bell said.

"Except ourselves," Buckley put in. "We've got to trust somebody."

"We've got six men," Bell repeated. "And the driver, who takes the stage to the mine. And everyone who sees him drive up there and back." He shook his head. "I don't know how we can keep it secret."

"Fred and I've been working on it," Dale Buckley said. "Every stage that leaves Deadwood is going to be driven to the mine, parked there for a few hours, then

22

brought back to town."

"But every stage won't be carrying gold," father said. "Do you see the possibilities of it, Jim?"

"I do," Bell said, smiling. "If the robbers want gold, they'll have to hit every stage out of Deadwood."

"Right," Buckley said. "And there won't be any more surprises because the shotgun guard will be looking for trouble every inch of the way."

"It's as foolproof as we can make it," father said. "We're going to try it, Jim, and if it doesn't work, we'll organize a vigilante committee and clean them out."

Jim Bell frowned. "A vigilante committee? That's a bad word to a lawman, Fred. Besides, where would you start?"

"I don't know how we can keep it secret."

"We're going to give this plan a whirl and see how it works out. A couple of weeks ought to tell." Father glanced at me. "I'm afraid that my son is going to be sitting in a hot spot during this trial. There is no doubt that the robbers will hit the stage, thinking there is gold on it."

"Can I say something?" I asked. No one seemed to have any objection. "Well, it seems that protecting the gold is all right, but you're going to have to get rid of the robbers. It's always struck me a little odd that none of them have ever been captured."

Jim Bell took that as a personal slight. "Look, Page, I do my best, but the trail always peters out near town. Your robbers are right out there walking up and down the street. But pick 'em out. You can't do it and neither can I." He blew out a ragged breath. "We're working against highly organized men. Cracking that bunch is going to be tough. I don't know how to do it, and I've been thinking of nothing else for months."

23

"The company can't stand many more losses like we've sustained," Dale Buckley said. "It's getting so I can't hire a man to ride shotgun for me; they all get tired of holding their hands over their heads." He glanced at me. "They never hit in the same place twice, and like I was told the other day, it's getting to be a contest to see if they run out of places before we run out of gold, or the other way round. One man always blocks the road with a drawn gun, and so far no shotgun guard has ever tried to find out who was hiding in the brush."

"Maybe he's alone," I said.

Jim Bell shook his head. "Not likely. It takes more than one man to cart off three hundred pounds of gold bars. No, I wouldn't argue the matter either."

"One more question," I said. "Why does the gold always go out on the night stage? It seems to me that if a guard could see a little something, he'd be able to do something a little quicker."

"We did that three months ago," Dale Buckley said. "Remember the shotgun that got killed? He could see and took a chance; it didn't work." His face took on a negative expression. "No, I'd rather have the odds in favor of the bandits surprising and getting the drop on driver and guard, than have them take a chance on a shoot out." He pointed his finger squarely at me. "Now you get this straight, Page. You have the clear drop on a man before you open up on him. I don't want you carted back to town dead."

"I'm against that myself," I said. "Well, when do we start?"

"Gabe ought to be here with the coach any time now," Buckley said. "How much will she be carrying tonight, Fred?"

"Seventy-five dollars worth of lead," father said.

"How come?" I asked.

"Just part of the plan to keep the robbers working overtime," Buckley said. "We couldn't send an empty coach, they're too smart for that. One look at the shallow ruts and they'd know she was traveling light. We'll hold off until next trip with the actual shipment." He slapped his desk. "The meeting is adjourned. And what was said here goes no further. Not even with your families."

"Naturally," father said, a little offended. We all went outside, and Jim Bell moved on down the street. The night was young, but all the saloons were doing a rushing business and he had his work cut out for him. Father lit a cigar and puffed on it for a time. Then he said, "Tonight's the one you'll have to worry about, Page. The stage has never been hit farther than twenty miles down the road. The robbers like Deadwood; they can lose themselves here so that we can't hunt them out."

"I won't be asleep, pa."

He grunted and puffed on his cigar. Gabe came down the street with the stage and drew up before the express office. Four passengers left the waiting room and got in, the mail pouch was passed up, and I climbed up on the seat with him, feeling pretty nervous and unsure of myself.

Father stood there, rolling his cigar from one side of his mouth to the other, then Gabe whooped to the team and we made a plunging run out of town.

There wasn't much of a moon and I didn't know the road very well but Gabe drove at a reckless pace, sliding around corners, sometimes clipping dirt banks with the rear axle stub. I couldn't see thirty feet ahead and it bothered me until I realized that any robber waiting ahead couldn't see either. Still he could hear us coming, and I didn't like to give any robber that much of an edge.

The trip was dusty and noisy, and the conversations Gabe and I had were shouted at the top of our lungs. He'd been held up four tunes now, always along this stretch of road, and he pointed out to me all the likely ambush spots; it was quite an education, and always with the promise I'd get to put it into practice any minute.

Trouble always occured between Deadwood and the Salt Creek stage station; I breathed a sigh of relief when we pulled in after a five-hour run. The lathered team was unhitched and I got down when Gabe said, 'Ten minutes here."

The passengers got down and I went into the station, a low log building. The station agent and two hostlers were changing horses, and the agent's wife served coffee and cold meat. She kept looking at me and at the long-barreled shotgun, then her curiosity got the best of her.

"Are you the new guard?"

I nodded. She was an attractive woman, a little plump, and showing lines in her face, but you expected that with hard winters and hot summers and a woman doing half a man's work all the time.

"You ain't much more'n a kid," she said and went to serve the passengers.

Gabe came over and leaned against the bar. "Sometimes we get through and sometimes we don't," he said. "I like the times we do better than the times we don't." His glance touched me. "I kind of like to have a talk with the shotgun. Kind of like to get a slant on what he's going to do. You know, so I can duck or stick my hands up."

"If I see the man first," I said, "better duck. Gabe, if I could wing one and take him to Jim Bell, there's a chance he'd talk. That's all we need to get a wedge into those robbers. Just one man who'll talk."

"That's ambitious," Gabe said and finished his coffee. We loaded and pulled out and I found I could relax a little. When we pulled into Jake Spade's station four hours later, the passengers were too tired or too sleepy to even get down. I gulped two cups of coffee to keep me awake, then we pushed on to Rapid City, arriving around noon.

It was a long fifty miles, and I slept until nine that night, took in the town, slept some more, and caught the morning stage back. By now I was feeling pretty good about my job, and there wasn't any doubt any longer about being able to handle it.

The coach was a mudwagon, not a Concord, with nine passengers inside, one riding beside the driver, and myself and Gabe stretched out on top. There was no shotgun on this run, seeing as how the only valuables carried were in the pockets of the passengers; the company liked to save money where it could.

I slept for the day was warm and sunny, and I'd just brace up against the luggage rails and let the swaying coach rock me. Around dusk the driver suddenly whoaed up and when I opened my eyes, Gabe and the others had their hands up. The bandit was standing beside the road, a rather short, shabbily dressed man waving a cavalry pistol.

The passengers were getting down and I thought that I'd better join them, but I didn't get a chance. The bandit pointed to me stretched out there and asked, "What ails him?"

"Dead drunk," Gabe said. "He can't take the stuff."

27

He put his hand on my chest as though to hold me there, then started to get down while the passengers lined up, the men swearing and the two women whimpering.

My Purdy shotgun was right there by my hand, and I don't honestly think I measured the chances at all; I just took them. He saw me come alive and he swung his pistol up as I whipped the shotgun around, and I think he fired a heartbeat ahead of me for I felt the bullet hit the coach. Then the ten gauge Purdy roared and he was just swept back off his feet and crashed into some nearby brush.

I don't know when he died because I didn't get down to watch him. Everyone except myself and the women crowded around, then a few minutes later, Gabe came back and climbed on top. My complexion must have been like old curd, but he didn't remark about it.

Gabe said, "Some damn fool who went broke and tried to get a new stake the hard way." He took out his chewing tobacco, bit off a piece, then handed it to me. "If you're goin' to get sick, there ain't no better reason than a man's first chaw."

He was right; the tobacco did make me sick, but we were moving by then and I lay over the rear end of the coach and no one knew it but Gabe, and he wasn't going to say anything.

The dead man was wrapped in a canvas and tied onto the boot in back; the driver thought we ought to make a full report of this to Jim Bell in Deadwood. I still clung to the idea that I'd shot one of the robbers, but I couldn't logically account for his trying the holdup so far from Deadwood, and alone too. It didn't set good with me, my killing him for the few hundred dollars he might have got.

We arrived in town around ten o'clock, and my father was waiting; so were Jim Bell and Dale Buckley. The passengers got down and hurried off; they always seemed to be an impatient lot. And the driver made his brief report.

Gabe and two other men carried the dead man inside, and Bell kept the crowd out. The canvas was unwrapped and father and the others had their look.

Bell asked, "Anyone know him?"

"His face is somehow familiar," Buckley said. "I think he worked for me last winter a hostler at Jake Spade's station. Have to check it to be sure."

"I'll do that," Bell said. He glanced at me. "You started earning your pay right off, Page."

"I'm not happy about it," I said.

"Don't be unhappy," Dale Buckley said. "The man held up a stage. No matter what reasons he had, he was a bandit." He reached over and pulled the canvas back across the man's face. "I'll make a report of this to the company. Bell, find out who he was and if he had a family." Then he clapped me on the shoulder and turned me toward the door. "Get some sleep. You're going out again tonight."

Father walked home with me and he didn't say anything until we cleared the traffic of the main street. "I don't think," he said, "that we ought to talk of this around your mother."

"Won't she hear about it?"

He shook his head. "She doesn't listen for those things." He walked a way in silence. "It must have been a hard thing. I can remember the war; it was a hard thing then. It always is, no matter what reasons you have, or the cause you support."

"It was over so fast I couldn't think," I said. "I can't

29

say whether I was scared or not, pa."

My father stopped and peered at me through the darkness. "Page, if I have a choice, I'll take the man who's a coward, but who cares about the things he does, rather than the brave man who doesn't give a damn. Now come on, let's get home. Your mother's worried enough."

Grandpa didn't hear the whole story until early afternoon of the next day. I was out back in the barn, mending some buggy harness when he came out, a bright glint of speculation in his eyes.

"Heard you done a man in last night," he said and sat down on an old saddlemaker's bench. "You meanin' to keep it a secret from your ol' gramp?"

"I didn't want to talk about it around the house," I said. "Guess I didn't want to talk about it at all. It made me sick, to think he died for just that. To think that I shot him down for just that."

Grandpa watched me as though he couldn't make up his mind about something. Then he said, "I remember rendezvous in '43. There was a big Frenchman there, always talkin', always botherin' a friend of mine. Two times this here fella was told to shut up, to go away, but somehow it just didn't soak in. Then my friend just up and pulled his blade and sunk it in his gizzard. We got to watch ourselves, boy. People ain't goin' to spend all their time teachin' us what to do. We got to do right by ourselves, or take what we get."

He had a point, one of life's hard truths, but it would take some time before I really accepted it. I said, "Grandpa, are you happy here?"

He smiled. "Boy, I got no choice but to be happy. If I wasn't here, where'd I go? Up in the hills to die like

30

some old he-bear too crippled up to fight for himself?" He shook his head. "It takes a man a long time to put aside fifty-five years of doin' for himself, and take the waitin' on of other people. Boy, there's nothin' I'd like more than to just know I was good for somethin'. It don't bother a man to die when he knows he's doin' somethin'. It only bothers him when he knows all that's left is the dyin'."

Father came around the house and into the barn. He said, "I just saw Jim Bell a few minutes ago. He wants to know if you can come to his office."

"What's wrong?"

"Well, I guess nothing. Except that he found out who the bandit was."

"So soon?"

Father shrugged. "This morning, a woman came to town looking for her husband. She talked to Bell, described him, and that was that."

"What does Bell want me for?"

"She wants to talk to you," father said. "Son, this isn't going to be easy, but it's what a man runs into now and then, talking to the ones that are left. Like last year when there was that slide in number six shaft. I think you'd better go do it."

"Arc you coming along?"

He shook his head. "You've got to do this alone."

I put on my coat and went uptown, all the time wondering what I'd say to her, or what she'd say to me. I knew I couldn't answer anything for her.

Bell's office was on a side street, with the jail behind, and I went on in. He was sitting at his desk and when I closed the door, a woman got up from the chair and looked at me. She was rather chunky, quite plain, and all the hard work in her life was, there to see in her face,

31

and in the roundness of her shoulders.

"You?" she said softly. "Why, you're just a boy."

Bell said, "Mrs. Anstadt, this is Page Sheridan, the shotgun guard for the express company."

She looked at me and then walked over to me and said, "He was all I had. Did you know that?"

"No, I didn't know it," I said. "I'm sorry."

"Why should you be? You didn't know him. He was just a foolish, desperate man with a gun in his hand, wasn't he?"

"Yes, ma'am. He was."

"What'll I do now? We were going to starve; that's why he tried to hold up the stage, to get some money. Now I'll starve without him."

I opened my mouth to say something, and Jim Bell shook his head. "Mrs.Anstadt, we found thirty-eight dollars on him. It's yours, of course."

She looked at Bell and frowned. "He had no money. How could he have gotten it?"

"I don't know. Maybe he met someone on the road and gambled." He shrugged. "I guess we'll never know." He reached into his desk and took out a doeskin money sack and counted out the thirty-eight dollars. "God knows it isn't much, but it'll buy you a ticket out of here."

He held it out to her and she hesitated, then took it. "Fifteen years, thirty-eight dollars. I wonder who came out ahead, marshal. He didn't, because he's dead. I didn't, I know." Then she turned to me again. "I wanted to see you, to tell you not to feel sorry, not waste your time."

"I'm still sorry," I said. "Believe that."

"You're a fool if you are," she said. "A man is what he is from moment to moment. What he's been doesn't count, and what he's going to be ain't worth a hill of beans. Just this moment, that's what we are, no more. My Amos was a bandit in his last moment. Don't waste your time feeling sorry."

She brushed past me and walked out. Bell sighed and sat down.

"A remarkable woman," I said.

"They all are, just because they're women," Jim Bell said.

"He didn't have a dime on him," I said. "Gabe told me that."

Bell shrugged. "She wouldn't take a handout. It was all I could do. I think the odd denomination got her, Page. Forty, fifty dollars, would have warned her; we rarely wind up with even amounts in our pockets. If you feel real touched about it, I'll split the sum with you."

"All right, after my first payday."

Bell took a bottle from his desk drawer and offered me a drink, but I shook my head. He poured one for himself, then leaned back and rolled a cigarette. "You won't be carrying lead tonight, Page."

"It won't make any difference to me," I said. "I still wish we made the run during the day though. I like a fighting chance."

"You're not using your head," Bell said. "Page, suppose you made your run in the daylight and you were carrying twenty thousand. For that much money, the robbers wouldn't take a chance on getting a man weighed down with buckshot. No, they'd put a rifleman in some high place, pot you out of the seat just before the rest jumped you. So you see, making the runs at night keeps that from happening. I guess Dale figures they'll catch the robbers sooner or later, and in the meantime he'd rather lose gold than men."

33

It was a sobering theory, one I hadn't really considered, and now that I'd heard it, I didn't consider all the advantages being on the robbers' side.

"Suddenly the night run attracts me," I said. There was no use hanging around Bell's office, so I got up and turned to the door. "Another conference at six?"

"Yes," Bell said and I went out.

When I got home, mother had some work laid out for me, and I did it just so I wouldn't be bothered with it later. While I was carrying in the firewood, I noticed grandpa on the back porch, carefully assembling an old Sharps rifle. At a glance I estimated the barrel to be thirty inches long, and the whole gun to weigh nearly twelve pounds. As soon as I finished, I went out and sat down on the porch He was running a wiping stick down the bore.

"Where can a body shoot around here?" he asked.

"About a mile out of town. Want me to hitch the buggy?"

He glared. "You gettin' smart with me? Boy, I've caught wild horses by runnin' 'em down, Injun style. I'll walk. You're welcome to come if you think you can make the trip."

I grinned. "If I can't, Grandpa, I'll let you carry me back."

He snorted like a prodded hog, and went in the house to get some shells. We cut away from town, walked for twenty minutes, and I must admit that he could cover ground like a deer. I just kept to the proper direction, but he was going off every which way, snooping around, crossing the trail, recrossing it; he walked half again as far as I did and didn't even get his wind up.

He finally picked a ridge, bellied down, sought out a target a good four hundred yards away, loaded the

Sharps and hit it square on the first shot. To tell the truth, I couldn't tell what he was shooting at until I saw the rock take on a white blaze where the slug flattened.

I guess he saw me squinting, for he said, "That's the good of book readin'. Ruins your eyes. Never read a word in my life, and I can see lice on a buzzard's back at seventy yards. You want to try a shot?" I took the Sharps and tried to sit up, but he scolded me with some irritation. "God damn it, that ain't a standin' piece! Shoot her on your belly and shoot far. Here, I'll show you."

He wiped out the bore between shots, which I thought was a waste of time, but there was nothing wrong with his shooting. He could hit a pie tin at four hundred yards, and I guessed a man at six or seven, which must have made him dangerous enough in his rip-roaring days.

Finally he got tired of banging away and rolled over on his back to stare at the sky. "Be you get lonesome one of these nights, I'd as soon go along as stay around the house. I like to be on the move. Stayin' in one place is hard."

"Well, I'd have to ask Dale Buckley, grandpa."

"What for? Can't this be between you and me?"

"I don't know," I said. "I'd hate to do something Buckley wouldn't like."

"Hell, if it's goin' to put you out, then forget it," he snapped.

"I don't think ma'd like it either," I pointed out.

He laughed. "Boy, *I* raised her. She didn't raise me. By golly, what do I have to do, buy a ticket on that stage?"

"You got any money, grandpa?"

He reared up, then got to his feet. "No, I ain't, but I'll get some. And by golly, you'll treat me respectful

35

'cause I'll be a payin' passenger."

He picked up his gun and empty brass cases and wiping stick and walked on home, not looking back once. I couldn't believe that he was angry at me, but I realized that he must be, for I had touched his tender pride, reminded him in one of the thousand possible ways that he was an old man and nearly useless.

There wasn't time for me to make up to him. I had eat and change clothes and go to the express office. Father was there, and as I started to close the door, Jim Bell came down the street.

I knew they were shipping gold because their expressions were more serious, more severe. Father said, "There's twenty thousand in the box, Dale. I expect you've filled out all the papers."

"Everything's been taken care of," Buckley said. "Jim, do you have anything you want to say?"

"Just that I'm going along this time," Bell said. "Inside the coach, as a passenger. If it makes any unauthorized stops, I'll be warned in time to get out and make a fight of it." He glanced at me. "The minute you hear me open the door, and cut loose, get off that seat and back me up."

"All right," I said. "You going to take a sawed-off?"

Bell shook his head and opened his coat, revealing a pair of pistols. "I couldn't hit a bull's ass with a shotgun if I had it pressed under his tail."

Buckley looked at Bell steadily, then said, "Jim, you've never gone along before. You never thought it would do any good. Can I ask what's changed your mind?"

"Page Sheridan changed it," Bell said. "He's the first shotgun you've had that I could count on to make a fight. Dale, I wouldn't want to end up standing alone

36

against the robbers. None of us know how many they are, three, six, ten—" He laughed. "I like living." Then he slapped his legs and stood up. "I'll meet you down at the end of the street. Tell Gabe to slow her down a little as he rounds the corner and I'll hop aboard. The less who see me get on, the better it will be."

"That's a good idea," father said. I could see that he was relieved, but that he wasn't going to let on about it. Frankly, I was relieved myself, because I knew Jim Bell; he could handle himself real well, and a sixshooter seemed to fit either hand.

Buckley consulted his watch. "Gabe will be in shortly. Shall we wait outside?"

They filed out, and I hung back to speak to Dale Buckley. "Does Gabe ever know what he's carrying, Dale?"

"No. Why?"

I shrugged. "I'm still thinking about the leak in the boat. The robbers always know when a shipment is going, and I'll lay you odds they know how much is in the boot before it's opened."

Buckley frowned. "We'll keep working on it, Page. We're bound to find out something, uncover something. It'll just take time, that's all."

"Looks like," I said and went out to wait for Gabe and the stage, and twenty thousand in gold.

CHAPTER 3

AT THE TIME IT WAS HARD TO SAY WHETHER I WAS disappointed or glad, but we arrived in Rapid City without incident; I turned the gold over to the express agent, saw it locked up in the safe, then went to the

37

hotel to get some sleep.

When I got back to Deadwood, I reported to Dale Buckley and went home. It was a Saturday and my two brothers were playing in the front lawn; they ran to me and Ralph carried my shotgun while Joe took my coat and blanket roll. I'd never been treated this way before and I guessed that it was the job; I was in a man's world now and it called for a different set of behavior rules.

Mother was in the kitchen and I gave her a kiss before turning to the cupboard. "Where's grandpa?" I asked.

"He got a job," mother said. She was vexed about it, I could see, so I didn't press her, just let her tell it her own way. "He insists on paying room and board. It's the most foolish thing I ever heard of."

I made a sandwich and sat down at the table. "Where's he working?"

"At the express company stable," she said, her lips tightly drawn. "Page, get him to quit, to come home."

"How can I do that? He wouldn't listen to me."

"I think he would," she said. "Try anyway."

"All right," I said, and finished the sandwich. Walking back uptown, I thought it over, and it really didn't surprise me none that grandpa had latched onto a job. I guess parents forget how much their children and old folks dislike a handout, even when it's given gladly, without thought of being repaid. People just have to pay their own way or lose their self respect, and I wasn't going to do anything to discourage grandpa.

I found him out back at the manure pile, loading a wagon. He had a sweat up and even though he saw me, he didn't stop until the wagon was loaded.

"Want some help?" I asked.

"You got your job, I got mine," grandpa said. "And don't stand there gabbin' and keep me from it." He cast the pitchfork into the manure pile and got up on the wagon.

"Where you goin'?"

"Out to the Cady place," he said. "Wherever that is."

I started to climb aboard. "I'll go along and show you."

He put out his hand against my chest and stopped me. "Boy, I found my way all through this country when there wasn't a soul to tell me north from south."

With one of those bursts of insight we sometimes get, I knew that I understood him, knew how to get along with him. I batted his hand aside roughly and said, "Why you cranky old fart, I was only going along for company. I don't give a damn if you got lost and never come back."

He grinned and motioned for me to get aboard, and then he drove out of town, taking the road south. He enjoyed his chewing tobacco, and he offered some to me, and I surprised him by taking it. Finally he said, "I guess your ma's vexed at me, huh?"

"She's not too pleased," I said. "But that don't bother you."

"That's right, it don't," he said. "A man's got to do what he feels like, and a woman's got to put up with it. It's the way the world's made." He shot me a sideward glance. "Heard you got through without bein' held up."

"Luck, I guess. Or maybe the robbers didn't know we were carrying gold."

He laughed. "They knew. Boy, it's their business to know. Why, there was a time when I made a fortune robbin' furs off one of the big tradin' companies. I knew when they had pelts and when they didn't. And I knew when a pack train was on the move. You got to know, boy. It's part of the business."

"I'll bet there'd be a sizeable cash reward for anyone

capturing those robbers."

He glanced at me. "How much do you think?"

"I don't know. I'd have to ask Dale. Maybe a couple of hundred dollars apiece."

"That's enough to set a man up proper," grandpa said and thought about it all the rest of the way to Cady's place.

Cady was a rancher and a dirt farmer; he never sank a shovel in the ground looking for gold, but he was getting rich just the same. While everyone was too busy digging to think ahead, Cady fattened his calves and brought in his garden, then sold his products in Deadwood, and got fancy prices to boot. He had a cluster of neatly painted buildings set in a small valley, with water running right through his property.

Grandpa wouldn't let me help unload the manure, so I went to Cady's back porch to talk. He was a wiry, dry-mannered man with a lot of common sense, and we talked about the robbers; it seemed that everyone had them on their mind.

"You run the whole shebang like you were kids," Cady said.

"Oh?" I said, putting the right inflection on it. What the hell did Cady know about it anyway?

He had a thick skin and hard-set opinions, and he ignored my remark. "What does Buckley have to know about the gold for?"

"Because it's shipped on his line," I said. "Besides, it doesn't take much of a brain to figure out that if he didn't know, someone at the mine could claim he shipped and that it was robbed, and collect the insurance from the express company. That would be a hundred percent profit."

"Don't you trust each other any better than that?"

"It's not a matter of trust, but of good business methods."

He laughed. "I'd fix it so that only one man knew, then if it was held up, the others wouldn't have to wonder how it got out."

There wasn't much sense in talking to Cady, and I was glad when grandpa unloaded so we could get back to town. Cady paid grandpa four dollars for the manure, and we started back.

Dale Buckley was waiting for me at the stable, and he was very impatient, even irritated. "Where the hell have you been?" he asked, before I could even get down from the manure wagon.

"Out to Cady's place," I said. "What's the matter?"

"I've been looking for you for an hour, that's what's the matter."

"So I go out to Cady's on my time off," I said.

Buckley could see the argument sprouting, and he passed it off with a wave of his hand. "I want you to take a saddle horse to Rapid City. The company notified me that the mint is shipping thirty five thousand in specie because we've got a gold surplus in the bank and a shortage of cash." He took out his watch, looked at it, then put it back. "If you don't waste any time, you'll get there a few hours before the stage is due to leave. They know you're coming, and I've got a horse saddled and waiting. Your shotgun and stuff is on the saddle; I sent a boy to your house for it." He clapped me on the shoulder. "Of course there's a thirty dollar bonus in it for you, Page. I never ask a man to work for nothing."

What can a man say when the boss asks him to work? I nodded and went into the company stable with Buckley; he had a rangy bay ready to mount. "This is a regular passenger run, so don't let on that you're

41

carrying money. Most of it's paper, in a locked strong box. Good luck, and get it here. The mine has a payroll to meet."

I can't say that the fifty-mile ride appealed to me, but I mounted up and cut out of town, and held to a good pace for the first four miles. Then I dismounted and walked the horse for twenty minutes, swung up and rode on. Some coffee and a plate of stew at the stage station made me feel a little more human, and I changed horses. The sun was going down and the road fell into deep shadows. Darkness cut my time down a little, but I made Rapid City with some hours to spare.

Enough anyway to get a bath and a bit of sleep.

Gus Ringold was the Rapid City agent, and he followed company rules to the letter. We went into his office, Ringold, myself, and the shipper's representative, a U. S. Marshal, and the safe was opened, the gold counted, the express box locked, and the key given to the marshal. Buckley had a key on the other end of the line, and once that lock snapped shut, the box was never to be let out of my sight.

I carried it out and put it in the boot, then mounted up. Ringold passed me the papers to sign, and as I wrote my name, I glanced at the passenger list, my attention immediately drawn to one name: Emma Buckley.

The passengers came out, and I got a good look at her, tall with rich brown hair, and a face rather cameo-like. I leaned over and said, "Miss Buckley?"

She looked up, to see who was speaking, and I detected an irritation in her expression. "Yes?"

"I'm a good friend of your brother's," I said. "He asked me to look after you."

"Really?" she said and stepped into the coach, leaving

me feeling like a damned fool. The door closed and the driver came out and hopped up. They were a swaggering, aristocratic lot, drivers, and you waited for them; there was no two ways about that.

We ripped out of town and I clung to my hat with one hand and the seat grab rail with the other; he was that kind of a driver.

This was the first daylight run I'd made, and I liked it; you see the countryside, and watch the road. We pulled into the first stage station at noon and I hopped down to open the door, thinking that I might thaw Emma Buckley just a little by gallantly helping her get down. But it was my kind of luck to get the wrong side, and an elderly, prune-faced woman said, "Thank you, young man," and took my arm.

I couldn't leave the stage and by the time I looked, Emma was going inside the station. So I figured I'd catch her coming out, but it didn't work out that way. A smiling, well-dressed lightning rod salesman had her on his arm and put her aboard. I got up and settled down to the next sixteen mile stretch

Within twenty miles of Deadwood, I began to feel more familiar with the land, and could accurately predict every turn in the road; I'd hunted birds all through that country and knew every swale and hogback.

I began to look ahead, so to speak, to see the road in my mind even before my eyes could see it, figuring just where it would be convenient to stage an ambush. Also I carried the shotgun in my hands now and never took my attention off my business.

Perhaps that's why I wasn't as surprised as I should have been when we rounded a tight switchback and found the man standing in the middle of the road. All I saw was the rifle he carried, and the handkerchief on his face. The driver's foot came down on the brakes, locking the rear wheels, and the coach slewed a little bit, skidding so that I was turned toward the bandit.

Thirty-five yards, that was the range, and he never got a chance to say, "Stick 'em up." I gave him the right barrel, cut him down, and hit the ground even before the coach stopped. The driver threw me the strong box and leaped down as a pair of six shooters broke loose from a thicket ahead. The bullets puckered the coach and the passengers boiled out, all talking at once. I rather expected the old lady to break up, but she surprised me; it was Emma who looked as though she were going to bolt.

"Turn the coach over!" the driver said.

I didn't understand why, but it was no time to argue. All of us pushed and lifted, and the Concord tottered, then crashed on its side.

"Inside," the driver shouted, and he didn't wait for the ladies to obey him. He just flopped a door open, lifted them and gave them an ungallant toss.

The shooting was getting serious now, but it was all from one side of the road, three men, I guessed, and armed with pistols. The bullets thudded into the heavy top of the coach and failed to penetrate, and now I understood the driver's desire to get it on its side. The top, floor, and ends are solid oak, while the side panels are light pine.

We had a pretty good box fort, and I saw that everyone got in before I tried it. The bandits had been shooting without effect, but now they understood our intent and got a little organization into their effort. When the driver dived inside, they peppered the coach, and he got hit, high in the thigh; I saw him jump, then fade inside, where he cursed steadily, unmindful of the women passengers.

Everyone was secure inside, except me, and as long as I crouched down I was safe, but not for long. They would soon cross the road up ahead, and then I'd be a nice target, crouching there.

I had to get inside, but they were also waiting for me to try it. So I gave it some thought and figured I'd stand a better chance if I went in shooting. I'd already slipped a fresh shell into the shotgun, while scrooched down, and I peered around the end of the coach, hoping to generally locate their positions. Things had turned off quiet. The dead man was crumpled up in the road ahead, and there was no sound; you could hear insects buzzing around.

Quite boldly I stood up, and immediately drew their fire. I spotted one man in an alder thicket, and put a load of buckshot in there. I didn't think I'd wounded him, but I'd broken his nerve. As soon as I popped out of sight, the shooting stopped, so I broke the gun, fed in another shell, and stood up again. I drew fire all right, but not much; they hadn't expected me to reappear so quickly. Letting go both barrels, I vaulted up and over and went into the coach, landing half on the lightning rod salesman,

The strongbox was still outside, but it was safe enough there; they'd still have to come in and get it and they couldn't do that until it was dark. And then we could get out of the coach without being seen.

The horses had been doing some thrashing in the tangle of harness. Now they broke loose and stampeded down the road, which pleased me because they'd head for the barn and then the station manager would know we were in a bind.

The driver was sitting up, and he'd wrapped his; leg with strips of his shirt. I said, "You get it bad, Curley?"

"Naw, I'll live, cuss it," he said.

Emma Buckley was crouched into a corner like a rabbit backed into his. burrow, and tears ran down her cheeks. The older woman's composure was worthy of admiration. She said, "Who's in charge?"

"I am," I said. The salesman looked like he had an objection, but he kept it to himself. "Be a couple hours until dark. We'll stay in here until then."

There was some luggage scattered about, and I picked up a heavy canvas traveling bag. The salesman said, "That's mine."

"I'll see that you get it back," I said and thrust the handle over the muzzle of the shotgun, letting it slide back to the wooden foregrip. Then I raised up through the open door and plopped the satchel down, using it as a shield and a rest. Immediately there was a burst of pistol fire and two bullets sank into the luggage, but didn't pass through. Ahead, on the road, about eighty yards' distance, one man made his dash across, and I must say that it was the best wing shot I ever made. He was in the clear less than three seconds, and moving fast, but I stopped him there, right on the edge.

I reloaded the gun and sank back inside.

The driver looked at me, the question in his eyes, and I said, "Two down, two left."

"Good boy," he said and closed his eyes and sighed.

The salesman said, "What do they want anyway?"

"Money," the old woman said. "Ain't that what everyone wants?"

"What a time for philosophy," the salesman said. He looked steadily at me. "My name's Reiner. And I was born in '47."

46

"So why tell me?" I said. "I'm not keeping a diary."

"I want something over my grave," he said. "Is that unreasonable? Why don't you give them the money?"

"I get paid not to give it away," I told him. "Why don't you sit back and relax? They can't get inside. And bullets won't go through the heavy wood." I gave him back his satchel. "There's a couple of slugs in there among your shirts. You can have them strung on a watch fob." I stood up and crouched there so my head wouldn't be exposed.

"Where are you going?" Reiner asked.

"Out," I said. "Along the road, in the brush somewhere. I can't stay in here because I can't see what's going on. Outside, I can keep an eye on everything."

Reiner grabbed my pant leg. "I'm unarmed!"

I still don't know why it bothered me. Maybe it was the note in his voice, the touch of panic there, the fear that I felt and kept pushed down. Anyway I hit him, hard and quickly, and he was flung back, his head rapping the top of the coach Emma Buckley gasped, and the old woman said, "I hope you didn't hurt your hand."

"I like you," I said and jumped out, hit the ground and dashed for the roadside. They took a few shots at me, and one of the bullets hit the stock of my shotgun, nearly causing me to drop it. I went into an alder thicket, rolled, and came to rest six yards away. My view of the other side was good, and I lay there for a time, listening to the buzz of insects, and watching the shadows get long.

This was one of those times in a man's life when things get shorn down to the bare facts, to just about all there is. You get to find out things about yourself that way. I had a man's growth, and a man's place to fill in

47

life; still, being young was a handicap. I simply lacked experience, so much so that just about anything I did would be the first time around for me.

I wondered how the bandits were taking this turn of events. What started out to be a slick-as-pie holdup had now cost them two men, and there'd be a third if he got careless and poked his head out to where I could get a shot at it.

The time eased by, slowly, as it always does when you want it to hurry, and the sun slid behind the hills while the shadows kept getting deeper and blacker. By the time the coach was just a smudge in the road, I realized that the robbers weren't going to break from their position.

But it was time for us to change. I left my place in the brush and went to the coach. "Curley? Let's get out of here. I've got a rock outcropping picked out where we can hole up."

"I'll buy that," Curley said, and pulled himself up to the door. Reiner and I got him out, and he hobbled around on his good leg.

I helped Emma out, and the other woman. "Let's keep our voices down," I said and hefted the strong box.

The place I'd picked earlier was on a hillside, about seventy yards from the road, a bare upthrust of rock. I led the way and Curley was supported by Reiner, while the women walked behind. Emma tore her dress on some brush and cried over it, but the old woman shushed her sternly, and I couldn't help but smile over it. It was like having my mother along, with her firm hand and mind, and that practical sense of reality that you find difficult to get along without.

My hole in the hill was an uncomfortable place, small so that one couldn't stretch out; we just crowded in the best we could, and I went over to stand by Curley.

"I figure the horses are in by now," I said.

"That's about right," Curley said. "You got a knife, boy?"

"No."

"That slug is giving me hell," Curley said.

Emma Buckley said, "I wish you wouldn't swear so much. You sound terrible."

Curley didn't answer her and I knew he bit his lip to do it. But I guess he understood how it was with these eastern-raised women; they were full of nonsense that had to wear off. And the Dakotas was just the place to wear it off.

Reiner said, "How does it feel to shoot a man?"

For an instant I was too surprised to answer him, then I said, "If the other two come after the strongbox, I'll hand you the shotgun and you can find out firsthand."

Curley laughed and fumbled through his pockets for some cut plug. "I hate to think of sittin' here all night, but if it's a choice of goin' down there and gettin' shot, I guess sittin' ain't so bad." He fell silent for a moment. "What bothers me though is this leg. If I don't get that danged bullet out, I'll get poisonin' for sure, and they'll have to take it off. Can't drive a stage with one leg."

"Has anyone got a knife?" I asked.

No one spoke, then Reiner said, "Will a penknife do?"

"We'll make it do," I told him. "But we'll have to have light. A fire is out. But there are side lanterns on the coach. The one on the high side ought to be unbroken. Probably a good share of the coal oil has run out, but there might be enough left to do the job." I took Reiner by the arm. "Go on down and fetch the lantern back."

49

"Me? Why me?"

"Because I told you to." I gave him a shove. "Hurry it up. You'll be safe enough." He hesitated, then left the rocky pocket. "I'm going to need some petticoats, ladies. If you please."

Emma said, "Are you going to—to cut that man's leg?"

"I'll probably butcher him proper and give him a scar for life, but I'll get the bullet out. All right, Curley?"

"I'm with you, boy." He sighed and leaned back.

The old woman took off her petticoat and gave it to me, then took Emma by the arm and shook her. "He ain't going to wait all night."

While Emma made up her mind, I took the one petticoat and tore it into strips; I figured on using the other one for a heavy pad, a compress to stop the bleeding.

Reiner came back with the lantern and I set it on the ground, then touched a match to the wick. It sputtered, then caught hold and burned steadily. It was a chore getting Curley's pants off, and Emma gasped and turned her head. The old woman knelt and said, "I've worked on my late husband from time to time, young fella." She tore open the leg of Curley's red flannels and exposed the wound.

There was some question in my mind whether I'd have the stomach for this or not, but there wasn't any choice. It was just one of those times when a fella had to do, and worry afterward.

"Curley, I'm going to have to give you a little belt on the jaw. Can't take a chance on you yelling out."

"Belt away," Curley said and turned his head to give me a straight shot. I uncorked one, all I had, and I nailed him squarely; he went as limp as a silk glove, and I took

50

the knife, passing the blade quickly through the flame.

I found the bullet with the point of the knife, imbedded well, and I had to cut to get it out. Curley bled a lot and my hands got slick and the knife grew difficult to hold, but the bullet came out, a round slug from a cap and ball. Still I was only half through and the nasty part was still to come. With the knife I pried open a shotgun shell and poured a good shot of black powder into the wound.

"Reiner, put something over his mouth when I tell you. He'll cry out when I light this." I got a match ready, struck it, then nodded to Reiner, who put both hands over Curley's mouth. The powder hissed and Curley tightened like a heavy spring; he yelled all right, but Reiner muffled it.

Then it was all over, and the woman said, "I'll do it now. You're a good boy."

"Thank you, ma'am. And I'd be glad to have you along anytime."

"I'm Mrs. Dance," she said.

"Page Sheridan." I stood up and found that my legs were cramped, then I glanced at Emma Buckley and found her staring at my hands. For a moment I couldn't understand the look of horror on her face, then I glanced down at them to see what fascinated her. They were covered with blood, and in the lantern they looked black, as though ink stained.

How did I know she was going to scream? I've never figured it out Maybe I saw the tightness in her neck, the breath she took, the way her mouth shaped up for the found yet to come. I only knew that I couldn't allow it, so I swung on her, with an open hand, and I caught her on the cheek, hard enough to knock her down. The scream turned into a little bleat and a gurgle, then she put her hands to her face and cried some more and I felt genuinely sorry for her.

Curley came around nicely, and he felt of the heavy bandage on his leg. I touched Mrs. Dance on the shoulder and said, "Will you take care of her? I had to slap her." I motioned toward Emma Buckley.

"I heard," Mrs. Dance said. "What else could you do?"

A lot of things, I suppose; there always are alternatives, but a man never thinks of them until afterward, until it's too late. I knelt by Curley and put a hand on his shoulder. "Feeling pretty rough?"

"I'll get over that," Curley said, his breathing hard and deep. "You burn it out good, boy?" I nodded and he seemed relieved. "I knew you'd do right. You got your man teeth early."

We had to wait, and it wasn't easy. I heard nothing from the road and I wasn't sure whether the bandits had left or not. At least they didn't have the money. Finally I turned around to Emma Buckley.

"Did I hurt you?"

She wouldn't answer me, and Mrs. Dance held her in her arms and patted her head. "She's getting her lessons a mite fast, that's all. But she'll be all right. I can tell."

"I didn't want to hit her," I said. "I really didn't."

"Many of the things we do we don't do because we want to," Mrs. Dance said. I thought she'd said all she was going to say, then she spoke again. "Four years ago in Arizona, I found my Daniel hanging in the barn with his tongue gone and his eyeballs hanging on his cheeks. That's the way the Apaches left him, and it was my own hand that put the bullet in his heart."

"God," I said, really shaken by this. "I could never have done that."

52

"Yes, you could have done it," she said softly. "You know the country, know how to do a thing when there's no other road to take." She reached out and patted my hand. "My son's like you. Perhaps you know him. He's the marshal of Deadwood."

"Jim Bell? I thought you said your name—"

"That's my son by my first marriage," she said. "You know him?"

"Very well. I consider myself a good friend of Jim's." I laughed softly. "It's some world. I mean, finding you on the stage, and—well, it's just some world, that's all."

We talked about a good many things in the long hours, then Reiner, who was keeping a lookout, reached over and tapped me, indicating that he wanted me to be quiet. I listened, then heard the sound of horses on the road, and the unmistakable sounds of a stage; you can't mistake those squeaking leather springs for anything else. They came upon the wrecked stage suddenly and sawed to a halt. There was a profusion of lantern waving then I heard, "Boy, where be you, boy?"

"In the rocks, grandpa!" I fumbled for a match and lit the lantern, and when they saw it, they came up, Jim Bell and Buckley, and two other men. Grandpa brought up the rear and he had his old buffalo rifle with him, and anger in his eyes.

"What the devil are you doing here, grandpa?"

"What am I doin' here? Hell, I was at the stage relay station when the horses come in." He looked at Curley, then bent and gave him a hand up.

There was a moment of confusion with everyone talking at once. Emma flung herself into her brother's arms and sobbed and Bell kissed his mother, then we all started down, Reiner and grandpa carrying Curley. The two other men wanted to take the strong box, but I wouldn't have any of it. The darned thing wasn't going to get out of my sight until it was unlocked in Buckley's office and the money counted.

"Did you find the two men in the road?" I asked, and Buckley shook his head. The passengers were in the coach, and Jim Bell came up.

"No, they must have taken them along. Too bad. We might have recognized them."

"Which is why they were taken along," Buckley said. "Well, they'll get buried in the hills someplace. We'll wait for next time, and a bit more luck."

Grandpa came over; he'd been having a look around. "Been gone two, three hours maybe. Looks like you got two and a half, son."

"What do you mean, grandpa?"

"Found some blood in the bushes over there." He pointed to the spot where I'd flung a charge of buckshot. "Likely you winged him. If that's so, he's going to be showin' it."

"There's a break," Buckley said. "Jim, you keep an eye out for anyone sporting a bandage, or laid up suddenly with 'sickness.' Better check with the doctors in town."

"There's eight thousand people in Deadwood," Bell said. "I don't know a tenth of 'em."

"Well put a couple of deputies on it," Buckley said, expressing some irritation. "Hell, if I have to, I'll offer three hundred dollars to the man who turns him up." He turned to the two men who had come along. "I want you two to stay here until morning. I'll send out some help with a team and you can bring the stage in." He reached out and gave me a cuff on the head. "All right, shotgun, let's go up with the box and get back to town."

"Who's driving?" I asked.

54

"Why, Page says he can drive. He can, can't he?"

"He's just trying to show off," I said, then tossed the box in and stepped up. "Come on, grandpa, see if you can keep us out of the ditch."

"I ought to box your ears," Grandpa said and climbed up. He got the stage turned around without dumping it over, but there were a few moments there when I thought we were through.

When we got straightened out, I said, "I'll bet ma's worried sick because you didn't come home tonight. Probably got pa out looking for you right now."

"I'm a free man," Grandpa said. "I go where I please." Then he laughed and reached out and slammed me one in the middle of the back. "Wasn't goin' to take the old man along, was you? Goin' to be the big cheese all by yourself, wasn't you? Ha! You see who's drivin', don't you? Got here after all, didn't I? Gettin' paid for it too."

"You're hopeless, grandpa."

"Yeah? But I ain't helpless. Show your ma that too, damned if I won't. She thinks I'm through, just good fer sittin' and such. Show her, I will. By God, come next spring, I may start lookin' around for a wife. I never did take one legal, you know?"

"One of these days you're going to bust a blood vessel," I said. "A man your age shouldn't do anything more'n stroke the dog once in awhile." I knew this would insult him, but he liked it. Some people are that way; they get suspicious if you talk nice to them. "What did you do, make up that story about finding the blood in the bushes just to impress the boss?"

He snorted like a gored sow. "By golly, you think I'm bluffin', you just wait. There's a johnny around with buckshot in him, and when I find him, it's worth three hundred dollars to me. Hell, I can go to California on that." He reached out and poked me again. "I do hate to say it, but you do fair for a young sap. Of course, that's the Page blood in you. Comes out every other generation, they tell me. Give it another thirty years and you could pass yourself off as a man so good people would never know the difference."

"Grandpa, I don't know how anybody could deserve you."

He laughed. "You don't, boy. Rare ones like me you got to earn."

CHAPTER 4

WHEN WE ARRIVED AT DEADWOOD I EXPECTED TO GO home and take a bath and crawl into bed, but it didn't turn out that way. Dale Buckley told me to wait in his office, and he took his sister home; she was a pretty well frazzled young woman. I sat in Buckley's office for a good ten minutes, just swinging my leg and whistling to myself; then Jim Bell came in in a big rush.

Bell said, "Now I want to hear this story from end to end, Page."

I told it to him, leaving nothing out, and he smoked a cigar and nodded and took notes in a little pocket book he carried.

"You didn't recognize any of them?"

"Nope," I said. "They had masks on and I wasn't about to go out there in the road and take a peek."

"Damn it," he said.

The door burst open and father came in. "Are you all right, son?"

"I'm fine," I said. "I suppose ma's in a sweat?"

"Not yet," father said. "But she'll read about it in the paper." He took off his hat and wiped his forehead. "Why the hell don't I get out of the mining business? Have you got another cigar, Jim? I left the house in such a rush that I forgot mine. Thanks." He bent over the lamp chimney for his light. "It's a miserable shame the two bandits weren't found. Of course they would have been recognized."

"Which is why they were carted off," Jim Bell said. "Fred, if we ever pull a mask off one of the bandits, we're going to know the man by sight, because we've seen him walking the streets of Deadwood."

"One is packing buckshot," I said, reminding him of the blood grandfather had found in the bushes.

"I'll make a round of the doctors," Bell said, "although I'm positive no one would be fool enough to go there." He sighed. "No, someone's digging those pellets out with a knife. Likely we'll never know who it was."

Dale Buckley came back; he pulled the window and door shades and slid the bolt. "It's been some night," Buckley said. "Page, you've earned your bonus." He went around his desk and sat down. "I'm a little disappointed we didn't get an identification. Still, I'm very pleased. Now the bandits know that we're not fooling and that a holdup won't be so easy."

"That kind of makes me a target," I said. "I've given them a big hunk of trouble, and now they'll be laying for me."

"Which is why we're staying to night runs," Buckley said. "I'm not going to have you potted off the seat by some rifleman." He took out his watch and looked at it. "It's late. Page, why don't you go on home and get some sleep. If the rest of you will stay a few minutes, we'll talk over the next shipment."

That didn't sound quite right to me, but I went out anyway, wondering why Buckley wanted to exclude me. Hell, I was in this as much as anyone and I felt that I deserved a front row seat in the planning. But I was too tired to argue with anyone, so I turned down the street toward home.

The traffic was thick; Deadwood never acknowledged late hours. Every saloon was brightly lighted and talk and laughter and music poured through the constantly moving doors. I brushed my way through the sidewalk traffic, intending to cut across a block or so down, where there was more room.

Three men came charging down the walk; they were drunk and loud and were swinging their arms, and to keep clear, I eased over to the buildings, meaning to let them pass. Just as they came abreast, I stepped off the walk to cross the alleyway, and someone grabbed me from behind.

The arm around my throat cut off my wind and my cry for help, and I was whirled into the darkness. A fist came from somewhere, caught me flush in the stomach, and the air gushed out of me. Cramps made my legs double up and all the strength went out of me. The man still choked me from behind, and two more battered me from in front.

I remember dropping to the dirt, and I remember a man saying, "Give up that job, kid. It's too dangerous for you."

Then they went down the alley and I remained on the ground, trying not to be sick. Perhaps fifteen minutes passed before I could breathe properly, and then it wasn't easy for my ribs felt like they had been caved in and my throat ached from the stranglehold.

I began to think about how smoothly this had been pulled off, and how convenient it had been for those three drunks to come charging along just at the right time. Then I hauled my thinking up short. Convenient, my foot! The whole thing had been planned, timed to perfection, and I'd fallen into it like some young rabbit blundering into a snare.

The idea that I'd been set up honed my temper to a fine edge, and I got up and rested with my back to the building wall. I knew I'd have a few sore places for a week or so, but I wasn't badly hurt, not enough anyway to keep me from looking for those three men who came down the walk.

I considered getting a pistol from Buckley, then decided not to; it wasn't my kind of a weapon and unfamiliarity could get a man into trouble. So I crossed over and made my way to Bozeman's Billiard Parlor.

Jay was behind the cigar counter and he smiled at me when I came up. "Have you been sleeping in the alley, Page?"

I glanced at my clothes; they were dirty. "Just resting," I said. "Jay, do you have an old billiard cue I can have?"

"Sure," Bowman said and gave me one that was split near the tip. "Going to practice your game?"

"I guess," I said and went out carrying the cue.

Swan Farrell at the hardware store cut the billiard cue off for me and I kept the butt end, and about twenty inches of the shank. "You must be going to take up bouncing," Farrell remarked.

"Going to try it anyway," I told him and went out to the street.

It took me nearly two hours to comb Deadwood, and I went from one place to another, looking, asking friends.

I wanted to know about three men, all in their thirties, all with moderate beards, all dressed like miners. And I didn't get very far until I came to George Lear's place.

Lear ran a dance hall, not the best in town, and he did his own hawking right there on the street. He was a small man, quick-witted, and very observant; there were few men in town that Lear didn't know by name, and none he didn't know on sight.

"That's the Henry boys you're describing," Lear said.

"Try the hotel, Page. They've come into a few dollars and are living pretty high on the hog."

"Thanks, George."

I made my way down the street and went into the hotel. Ronny Searle was on the desk; we'd gone to school together, so I felt that I could ask straight out and get a good answer.

"Ronny, have you got the Henry boys registered here?"

"Three brothers?" He nodded. "Room 16 near the end of the hall."

"Describe them."

Ronny Searle frowned. "Well, Deke's the oldest. Thirty-five or so. The other two are twins, I think. All about the same build, rather dark, with short beards. They're a noisy bunch. Dirty too. Sleep three in a bed."

"That sounds like the ones," I said. "Ronny, let me have your pass key?"

He reared back a bit. "I couldn't do that!"

"For old times' sake?"

He laughed. "I'd get fired and I need the job. Sorry, Page. Can't do it."

"Thanks anyway," I said and went up the stairs to room sixteen. It occurred to me then that I should have asked Ronny if they were in, but I considered it too much trouble to go on downstairs. I rapped on the door with my knuckles and heard a man get off the bed.

The moment he opened the door I knew I'd found my man, and he recognized me too. Only I moved and he didn't. I jammed the butt end of the billiard cue into his gut with enough force to knock him out. He fell back into the room and jarred the whole upper floor when he hit. His brothers were stretched out on the bed; they had been asleep but now they woke with a bound. One snatched a pistol from a nearby holster and I swung the billiard cue, knocking it from his hand. The damned thing hit the wall and went off with an ear-shattering noise, then both men piled into me.

I opened a six inch split into one's head and dropped him there, but the other caught me with a looping right and knocked me half into the hall. The door of the room next down the hall opened and I caught a glimpse of Emma Buckley's frightened face; I had no more than a glance, for the remaining Henry brother was coming after me, and he had a Greene River knife in his hand. I parried his lunge by knocking the blade aside, but I didn't knock it clear of his hand. He made a backhand slash which I blocked by raising the cue, and he just whittled four inches off it then and there.

The backhand slash left him open for a second and I brought the cue down, not aiming at the knife, but for his forearm. And I caught him squarely and heard the bone break. He howled and dropped the knife and I cracked him alongside the jaw, taking him down like a sledged steer.

The gunshot and the noise was going to attract a crowd; I could hear them in the lobby. And I didn't want to be around when they came up the stairs. I dashed for the back stairs and found it barred and locked. Silently I cursed Ronny for doing too god a job.

Then Emma Buckley said, "In here! Quick!"

For a fact I'd forgotten her standing there. Quickly I ducked into her room, and she closed and locked her door as men ran up the stairs. There was quite a commotion in the hallway, then someone knocked on her door.

Emma said, "What do you want?" Who is it?" She sounded badly frightened and I wasn't sure whether she was putting it on or not.

A man said, "Lady, there's been some trouble. Did you see it?"

"I wouldn't open my door for anyone!" Emma said. "Go away!"

I heard the man grumble something about silly women, then he turned from her door. She faced me and put her finger to her lips, then motioned for me to sit down. There was only one chair, an old platform rocker with brass caps on the arms and I sat in it.

Emma wore a heavy robe over her nightgown, and from the disturbed bedcovers I knew she had been trying to sleep. Very softly she said, "You're a violent person, aren't you?"

"I thought Dale took you to his house," I said.

"You're changing the subject," she said. "He thought the hotel would be better tonight. Aren't you going to answer me?" She folded her hands demurely. "You picked that fight. Why?"

"It's a long story," I told her. The noise was dwindling off in the hallway. The Henry boys were coming around; I could hear one of them swearing steadily, and I felt a little embarrassed for Emma Buckley.

She said, "I acted disgracefully once in front of you.

I'm not going to do that again. I've made up my mind."

I knew she meant that because she was that kind; you could see the stubbornness in her eyes and in the set of her jaw. She'd made up her mind all right.

"There are a few people in town who might think it a bit improper for me to be sitting here, with the door closed, and you in your nightgown."

She hadn't thought about it just that way; I could tell by the way she blushed. But she wasn't going to be stampeded into anything either. "I'm not going to say anything if you're not," she said.

"I'm great with secrets," I said. "How old are you, Emma?"

"That's an impertinent question." Then she smiled. "I'm nineteen."

"Don't you mean, going on seventeen?"

"It isn't polite to dispute a lady's word."

I laughed. "Emma, Dale told me." He really hadn't, but it was enough to jar her.

"All right, seventeen then."

The hall was quiet now so I got up and went to the door. After standing there with my ear to the panel, I slid the bolt and took a look. There was no one in sight, and as far as I could tell, the Henry boys were gone from their room.

"Thanks for the refuge, Emma." I thrust the sawed off billiard cue in my belt.

She got off the bed and came to me. "Where are you going now?"

"Why I thought I'd go find the Henry brothers."

"For heaven's sake, why?"

I reached out and patted her cheek. "So they'll worry some. A worried man makes mistakes. I believe the Henry boys are part of the robber gang, and if I worry them, it might pass right on up to the leader. He's the one we want to get most of all."

"Please be careful That sounds silly but I mean it. You have a very dangerous job."

"The pay is good though."

I closed her door and stood there until I heard the lock click, then I went on down the stairs to the lobby. Ronny stared at me, then said, "Where the devil did you come from? I know you didn't go down the back because I checked the door."

"Why, I just ducked under the bed in the Henry brothers' room," I said. Ronny Searle was easily impressed, and he just shook his head and laughed.

"I always said you had more guts than brains, Page. The Henry boys left. Two of 'em were in pretty bad shape." He pointed down the street. "Deke was taking them to the doc, I think. They both needed it, one with a head cracked open and the other with his jaw laid bare. How come you went and picked the fight?"

"A grudge," I said and left the hotel.

There were only three doctors in Deadwood; the fourth one had taken the gold fever several years back and we hadn't heard much from him since; I went to Doc Wyatt's place first because it was on the main street. He was asleep and got sore as hell because I'd woke him; he hadn't patched up anyone since seven o'clock.

And that had been a miner with a smashed foot.

Doctor Lane lived on the east edge of town, and his wife told me that he'd gone out around eight to deliver a baby, and hadn't come back yet.

So when I knocked on Doctor DuJoir's door, I had my billiard cue in hand. He stared at it, then at me, then said, "Are you going to hit someone?"

64

"Did the Henry brothers come here tonight?" I thought I heard a movement inside, as though a man were standing just inside the door of his office, which was hidden from my view.'

"No, they haven't been here," DuJoir said.

I thought he was lying and pushed him aside, but before I could step in, Marshal Jim Bell showed himself. "I've been asking the same question, Page." He looked at the bloody billiard cue. "Been having yourself a time, haven't you?" He came to the front door, touched Doc DuJoir on the shoulder, then propelled me outside. "Come on, I'll walk home with you before you get into any more

CHAPTER 5

I COULDN'T TELL WHETHER JIM BELL WAS SORE AT ME or not; he steered me down the path to the street and there stopped. "I heard about the ruckus you raised at the hotel. You mad at the world?"

"I got kicked around in an alley and I didn't like it," I told him.

"So you got even. Will you leave the police work to me and go on home?"

"Then you'd better find Deke Henry's brothers. They need a doctor."

"That's exactly what I'm doing," Bell assured me. "Page, will you go on home now and leave it to me?"

"I want to be called when you find them," I said. "And I don't care how late it is."

"All right, all right," Bell said and gave me a little shove.

There wasn't much percentage in argument; he was a

65

stubborn man when he set his mind to it. So I went on home. Father and mother were in the parlor; she was working on some knitting and he was reading some reports.

He looked around when I came in. "Where the devil have you been?"

"Uptown," I said.

He got out of his chair, and came up to me. "Now the question I asked might possibly suggest to you that I wanted a more specific answer. You may be earning good money as a shotgun guard, but you're still my son and living under my roof, and if I have to, I can take you down a peg or two."

He hadn't talked to me like that for some time and I didn't want him to go any farther with it now. "I had some trouble," I said. "But Jim Bell's taken care of it."

Mother raised her head and looked at me. "A fight?"

"Well, I wouldn't say—"

"You don't have to say," she said. "Come in here and sit down." She kept looking up at me until I obeyed, then she put her knitting aside. "Page, I think you've proved that you're becoming manly. Now will you give up the job?"

I looked at my father. "Is this your idea, sir?"

"No, but I can't say that I disagree with her. What was the fight about?"

"Just a disagree—" He was getting that look on his face again, so I made a clean breast of it, although I talked down the idea that anyone was trying to discourage me, or make me quit Dale Buckley. "It's a tough town, dad. You've got to expect a little trouble now and then."

"I have trouble all the time," he said. "But it's out in the open. Where's your grandfather?"

"Gosh, I don't know. I thought he was here, in bed."

"He hasn't been home for two days," mother said. "Fred, I'm just not going to have it, this ramming around all over the country. People will start talking and I just won't have it. I wanted to give him a home, not a—a headquarters."

"I'll have a talk with him as soon as possible," father said. He pointed his finger at me. "And I wouldn't encourage him, if I were you."

"Why should I do that? He can take care of himself."

"It's not a matter of taking care of himself," mother snapped. "He's an old man and I wouldn't be surprised if he wasn't a little funny in the head at times." She bit her lip. "That's a horrible thing to say, I know, but we've got to face the facts. Don't you agree, Fred?"

"Oh, I think facing the facts is wonderful," father said.

She made a disgusted sound with her lips. "I get a lot of help from you. Both of you. Go to bed and don't forget to wash. I don't enjoy scrubbing the pillowcases."

I figured that she was more worried than irritated; she always turned cross when she worried, as though she were ashamed of it and didn't want people to think it was a weakness. So I washed and got into bed and lay back, thinking about the Henry brothers. Could be I'd bought a smear of trouble there, but I really didn't care. I still wanted to question them and find out who'd been in that alley.

Sleep came up on me without me realizing it, and the next thing I knew, someone wag clamping a hand hard over my mouth while the other held me still.

Then Wind-River Page said, "Easy there, sprout. Make nary a sound now."

I relaxed and he took his hand off my mouth; a good

thing he'd put it there or I'd have yelled out for sure. "What are you sneakin' around for, grandpa?"

"Sneak's my middle name. Quiet as a breeze, that's me. If I wasn't, I wouldn't be here." He chuckled. "Didn't think it was proper to wake anyone else. I found them fellas you beat up at the hotel."

"Where?"

"Oh, seven, eight miles out of town." He sat on the floor near the bed. "After the fight, I tagged along at a proper distance behind. Two of 'em was real bad hurt and I figured they'd look for a doc."

"They didn't go to any in town. I checked."

"True enough. They went to this fella's claim. I Injuned up to the window for a look. He's a doc, or he was once, 'cause he had all the fixin' in a leather bag."

I got out of bed and started to pull on my pants. "What time is it, grandpa?"

"Oh, nigh three in the mornin', I'd say. Figured you'd be rarin' to go. I got your shotgun out back, and a horse for you."

"You're all right, grandpa."

"All right? Hell, I'm the best there is, the hair on the dog, the grunt in the hog. I guess you don't think I'm on my last legs now, do you?"

"You'll fall apart any day now," I said and finished dressing.

I carried my boots in my hand and put them on when I got outside.

The old scout had the horse tied in the alley, and he handed me my shotgun. I said, "Ma's mad at you for not staying home."

"She'll get over it. Women is always mad about somethin'."

"Where's your horse?"

68

He chuckled. "Told you once a horse was good for pullin' a wagon and for eatin', when there's nothin' else. You just follow me, sonny, and keep your powder dry."

We skirted the town after leaving it and grandpa found a narrow winding trail leading into the hills. He followed it at a dogtrot for nearly an hour, then sat for a few minutes to take a chew of tobacco.

"How far?"

"'Bout the same," he said. "Goin' to be close to dawn by the time we get there." He got up and grabbed a handful of the horse's mane and flipped aboard. Before I could say anything, he said, "Just to save a bit of time, that's all. Let's go."

I let him have the lie. After all, he'd made two trips and had a right to be tired. He kept pointing out the way to me; it was not completely unfamiliar country, although I tried to stay out of it. These miners got touchy about their claims and a man could pick up a rifle bullet mighty easy by accidentally trespassing.

Finally we stopped and I could see lamplight shining through a dirty window. I tied up the horse and we went the rest of the way afoot, grandpa in the lead. We eased forward and raised up to look in the window. The two Henry boys were still there, sleeping on the floor, but Deke Henry was gone. I could see the third man moving back and forth; he kept passing out of view and I got the notion that he had someone in his bed that he was tending.

Grandpa put his lips close to my ear and said, "What you want to do?"

"I want to take those two Henry boys back to Jim Bell."

He nodded. "See the door? The latch ain't pinned. I'll

go on around and bust in that way. You cover me from here. They won't be looking for that."

"All right, grandpa. Be careful, huh?"

He squeezed my arm. "I'm old, ain't I? I got that way bein' careful." He moved away from me as silently as a ghost, and I thought of what a miserable business it would be to have him stalking me.

I cocked the shotgun and waited, watching the latch on the door. When I saw it slide open and the door flung wide, I poked the muzzle right through the window. A good thing too because one of the Henry boys was sleeping behind the opened door, out of grandpa's range of vision, and he woke and snatched up a gun.

Deliberately I put the load of buckshot right over his head, and he got the idea fast and dropped the pistol. Grandpa was well into the room now and had them covered with his buffalo rifle; I dashed around the corner and stepped inside.

I saw the man on the bed, a bloody bandage around his chest, and the man who had been tending him just stood there, not giving anyone any trouble. I'd seen him before; he was the doctor who'd given up his Deadwood practice to dig for gold.

"Everybody stay still," I said and walked over to look at the man in bed.

"He can't help you," the doctor said. "He's dead."

"But you're not," I pointed out.

He sighed. "But I could be if I did anything foolish, which I'm not about to do."

"You're so right," I said. I motioned toward a chair. "You sit down over there. What's your name?"

"Charles Blake."

"A doctor?"

"When I'm not working my claim," he said. Blake

70

was a very thin man, not large either. He sat there, calmly looking at me. Now and then he darted a glance at grandpa.

The two Henry boys remained in a sitting position and I collected their pistols. One wore a heavy bandage around his head while the other had his lower face swathed and bound.

"I gave you boys a rough time, didn't I?"

"We'll pay it off," one said.

"Which one are you?"

"Mort. He's Clyde. What the hell do you want with us?"

"Who got me in the alley last night?"

Clyde said, "Did someone get you?"

"Someone got you," I said. "It can happen again. What's to stop me from beating your head off right now?"

Blake said, "That's an inhuman thing to say."

"Shut up! You're in this to your ears."

"I hardly think so," Blake said. "These men are patients of mine. I don't mind picking up a dollar or two once in awhile. I'm not getting very rich off this mine you know."

I turned to Charles Blake, and pointed to the dead man on the bed. "I don't suppose it aroused your curiosity as to how he got that buckshot pellet in him."

"So you know it was buckshot." He looked at my shotgun. "And I take it you put it there? You could be arrested for shooting people."

"Not when they're busy holding up the stage. You could have sent word to Jim Bell that you treated that man."

"I could have," Blake said calmly. "And I would have except that I had no chance. Mort and Clyde showed up

71

with their brother and needed immediate attention."

"And you had no idea they were in with the bandits?"

Blake laughed. "Sonny, you're insane."

"We're gettin' nowhere," grandpa said. "Let me put some fire on 'em."

"Grandpa, you can't do that." I motioned for Mort and Clyde Henry to get to their feet. "We'll all go in town and talk it over with the marshal."

"What about my claim?" Blake asked. "Who's going to watch it?"

I laughed at him. "You just said you wasn't getting rich off it, so why worry about it? Besides, if you're as innocent as you say, you'll be back by nightfall."

"These two men aren't well enough to ride," Blake said. "For God's sake, I know you have a point to what you say, but be reasonable about it. One of you can remain here and guard them while the other goes for the marshal. Now that makes sense, doesn't it?"

"You sound pretty innocent," I said, and was halfway convinced by his sincerity. "All right, we'll compromise. Grandpa, you take these two back to town and I'll stay here with the kind healer."

"They're too badly hurt to ride!" Blake shouted.

"You're overselling that point a little," I said, again on my guard. "They came alive damned suddenly when grandpa opened the door, and they managed to ride up here in a lot worse shape than they're in now."

There must have been a finality in my voice for Blake only let his hands drop against his thighs and sat down. Grandpa said, "Come along, boys, and if you want to get to town alive, give me no trouble. I ain't killed a man for seven or eight months and I'm gettin' the itch again."

I was going to tell him to be careful, but I didn't want

to insult him in front of anyone, so I sat down near Blake and grandpa went out. The Henry boys had horses, which made the traveling a little easier, and grandpa took mine.

After we listened to them ride away, Charles Blake said, "I think I'll put all this down to the impetuousness of youth."

"Whatever makes you happy," I said.

We sat there for nearly an hour and watched the sun come up. Then Blake said, "Is it all right if I blow out the lamps. I don't have the coal oil to waste." I nodded and he moved around, snuffing out the lights. He was a very casual man and nothing so far had ruffled him; hc presented the appearance of patient innocence, and I decided to go along with him, to see what would happen.

I began to lounge in the chair and complain about being hungry. Blake said, "I could fix up some breakfast. Backfat and biscuits?"

"Nothing would taste better," I said, and sat there while he stoked up the fire and put on the skillet. I watched every move he made with suspicion. He sliced the meat, then said something about being extra hungry and diced some more, a lot more than two men could eat without getting a bellyache.

He tried me out by putting out the plates, moving pretty close to me a couple of times, and when I let on that I didn't care, he kind of took heart. Now I've seen my mother dish out bacon and the like a thousand times, and she always loads the plates at the stove so as not to have to handle the hot cast iron skillet. But Charles Blake brought the skillet to me, and I watched him closely.

He held it close to him, bracing his wrists against his

waist, and I actually sensed when he was going to throw the grease. I moved just as it left the skillet. A few drops got me, bit into me, but that was all.

I used the shotgun butt on him, caught him right alongside the head with it, and dropped him bleeding to the floor. Then I said, "Yeah, you're innocent all right." Then I picked up the spilled sidemeat and ate my breakfast.

CHAPTER 6

SEEING THE LOOK ON JIM BELL'S FACE WHEN GRANDPA marched those two thugs in and had them locked up was a pleasure denied me, but I figure that I made up for it when Bell and grandpa came to Charles Blake's diggings.

Bell was highly agitated as though he resented my interference, and I put it down to his desire to do a good job. He came into the cabin and said, "Page, what's the damned meaning of this?"

"I want him arrested. He's part of the outlaw gang."

"Hell, I just locked up two men on that charge," Bell said.

"Now you've got three," I told him. Then I saw Bell looking at the lump on Blake's head and explained it before Blake could. "He tried to jump me so I let him have it." I considered this in itself evidence. "Would an innocent man do that?"

Charles Blake smiled and shook his head. "Marshal, what would you do if a madman entered your house? Of course I jumped him. The boy's a lunatic and *he* ought to be locked up. But then, I've said all I'm going to on the matter. Marshal, I demand to be arrested and incarcerated in jail until a trial can be arranged. And when I'm acquitted, I'll prefer charges against this madman. People have a right to be protected against his kind."

I shouted, "You're not going to believe him, are you?"

Jim Bell said, "Page, we'll let the judge decide that, or a jury." He took Doctor Blake by the arm. "Come along, sir. Can you make it to town?"

"I could make it to the gates of perdition," Blake said, "if I was assured that there this moron would get his comeuppance." He glared at me and went out, and Bell motioned for grandpa and me to come along too.

While Blake was saddling his horse, Jim Bell said, "Son, I don't know what I'm going to do with you. Didn't I tell you to keep out of this and let me handle it?"

"Jim, you know I'm right in capturing these bandits."

"Will you let me exercise due process of law? Now you go on back to town. Stop off at my place and wait there. I want to talk to you, and for the last time."

"All right," I said. "Come along, grandpa"

We started down the trail and I was in a sour frame of mind; this wasn't working out the way I'd planned at all. But I was sure Jim Bell was right; he had to go according to the law. Which I thought was a danged shame.

When we got to town, grandpa said, "I'm goin' home. Likely I'll get hell, but I'm goin' just the same. Learn from me, son. Any woman will give you hell; it's a law of nature, so face up to it and get it over with."

"You've got me in a devil of a mess," I said.

"I got you in?" He laughed and rode off.

Mrs. Dance was sweeping down the porch when I

75

dismounted. She looked at me for a moment, then smiled as though she suddenly remembered me. "Why, it's that nice young man who works for the stage line. I thought you'd forgotten me."

"No ma'am." I walked to the porch. "Marshal Bell wanted me to wait here for him."

"Then you come right in. I've got cookies and buttermilk."

I wasn't in a mood to care for either, but I didn't want to hurt her feelings or explain mine, so I sat down at the kitchen table. She'd already put a woman's touch to the place, mostly with broom and mop.

"My son talks about you considerable," she said. "He thinks you have a grand future, perhaps as a peace officer."

"I hadn't considered it as a career," I said. "After all, I'm pretty young."

"What's age got to do with bein' a man?" she asked. "I've known grown men of fourteen, and boys of fifty. Those are good cookies, aren't they?"

"Yes, very good," I said and ate another to convince her that I meant it.

"Have you seen that little dear who came in on the stage?"

"Briefly," I said.

"I do hope she's all right. Sensitive, you know."

"She's learning," I told her.

We chatted about this and that for an hour, then Jim Belt came home and motioned for me to come in the parlor. "Sit down, Page." He paused to roll a cigarette. "Well, I've got three men in jail on your say-so. I take it you'll sign the complaints?"

"I certainly will," I said, thinking that this would make him feel better.

76

But it didn't.

"Thought you'd say that." He leaned toward me. "Page, what have you got in the line of proof?"

"The dead bandit in Blake's cabin."

"Blake's a doctor. He'd treat all who needed it. That's not proof."

"He jumped me."

Bell shook his head. "He explained that. Sounds logical to me."

"All right, what about Mort and Clyde Henry?"

"What about them?"

"They chivvied me into the alley."

Bell said, "Page, they claim they know nothing about it. Look, Blake's hired a lawyer, and since the Henry boys are broke, he's taking care of their defense too. Judge Wayne's agreed to sit on the case at ten o'clock in the morning, unless you want to drop the charges."

"Give me one reason why I should."

Bell smiled. "Aside from your damned mule stubbornness, I'd say you'd never make the charges stick."

"Then make the Henry boys and Blake talk!"

"How? By beating them?" He shook his head. "Page, they'd get on the stand and tell the judge they confessed under duress. I'd be in trouble then."

I was getting sore about this. "Then you'll do nothing?"

"That's all I can do, nothing." He got up and slapped my shoulder. "Page, Dale Buckley and your dad want to see you in Buckley's office. I told them I'd send you along as soon as we'd had our talk."

"I suppose they want to light into me too."

"They want to talk sense to you, the same as I do. It might be a good idea if you'd listen." He walked with me to the door. "Page, don't get sore at them. They're up on you both in years and in experience. You tried your best, and your intentions were good. Let it go at that and just ride shotgun, huh?"

"Maybe I'd better," I said.

He gave me another friendly slap on the back and I went down the walk thinking that that Jim Bell was all right. He'd kind of bawled me out, but in a. nice way, and I knew I wouldn't hold it against him.

The main street was so clogged with traffic that I had to take my horse around in the alley to find a place to tie him, and I went in the express office by the back way. Dale Buckley and dad were talking and they stopped when I came in.

"I've got a few things to say to you," father said, and I knew what was coming, a lot more than a few things.

But Dale Buckley stepped into the breech. "He's my employee, Fred, and I'll handle it if you don't mind." He folded his hands and looked at me steadily. "It seems that my attorney is going to have to appear in court tomorrow. What kind of a case does he have?"

"Not a very good one, I'm afraid," I said.

"Oh?" Buckley's eyebrow raised slightly. "But there are three men in jail. What are we going to do now, arrest all who arouse our suspicions? Defend ourselves in civil suits for false arrest? There's a law that protects people."

"Look, I didn't mean to get you all in a jam!" I said. "But I still think I've got three of the bandits in jail. Now maybe they're going to be set free, but not for long. They'll be caught again, and the next time I'll have proof."

"They may be caught," Buckley said, "and they may be confronted with evidence, but you won't gather it."

He wasn't as gentle as Jim Bell, and it hurt me, hearing this from a man I'd thought was my friend. So I let a little temper out, just to give him a taste of it. "It seems to me that you're not so all-fired anxious to get to the bottom of this as you say."

He went a little white around the mouth and I had a feeling I'd put it too strongly. Father said, "Your mouth is getting pretty big, boy."

"Now keep out of this, Fred." Dale Buckley stood up. "I'm going to tell you something, Page, and I want you to take the wax out of your ears and listen good. I have enough trouble now without having some young fool ramming around the countryside accusing people when he has nothing to back it up. Now you're on the payroll as a shotgun guard, and by God, if you don't stick to your job and leave the rest to someone else, I'll fire you altogether."

Father thrust his voice in before I could spout off something I'd regret. "Who found the Henry boys and Blake?"

"Grandpa did," I said.

"I'm going to suggest to grandpa," father said, "that he either sit on the porch or go squirrel hunting and leave this business to Jim Bell. And if he's got the sense of a drunk Indian, he'll take my advice to heart. And don't you say anything to him either. I'll do my own talking. Clear?"

"Yes, it's clear. Is there anything else?"

"No," Buckley said. "But you be in court in the morning. I want you there to hear what's said, and to think about it afterward. And Deke Henry's been saying around town that he wants to settle with you for this, and a few other things."

"He doesn't scare me."

"Then he ought to," Buckley said. "You need a good scare."

I got out of these before I said any more. It would serve them both right if I'd just up and quit.

Grandpa was sitting in the back yard when I got home and I went out to talk to him. He looked at me and said, "Well, you've still got your hide."

"How's yours?"

"Bleeding," he admitted. "Your ma ripped me up one side and down the other. What you think I'm sittin' out here for? She won't come out here and jaw me for fear of the neighbors hearin'. The only safe place on the property." He took me by the sleeve. "How about you goin' in' and fetchin' out m'blankets? I'll just camp here a spell until it blows over."

"She wouldn't let you do that, grandpa."

"A woman who's mad'll do anything," he said.

Mother came to the back door and called to me. "Page, you come here."

I went to the porch

"Page go tell your grandfather to come in the house."

"Why don't you just yell at him, ma?"

She stamped her foot. "Don't give me any sass. I want him to come in the house. The idea, sitting out there in the middle of the yard like an old Indian!"

"Well, I don't think he wants to come in, ma. As a matter of fact, he wants me to bring out his blankets."

She bit her lip and wadded up the hem of her apron. "Oh, the cantankerous old fool! What does he want, everyone in town to talk about me?" She brushed past me and stalked across the yard. Grandpa got up when he saw her coming and acted as though he were ready to put up his hands in defense. "Dad, will you come in the house?"

"Be you goin' to jaw me some more?"

"Oh, for heaven's sake, come in." She glanced toward the neighbor houses and so did I; we both saw curtains flutter down and knew that we had plenty of witnesses. This distressed mother; she hated a public row, and I guess it was just too much for her, because she began to cry.

Grandpa said, "Since it means that much to you, I'll come in." And as he passed, he said, "Forget my blankets, boy. When a woman cries, it's all over."

"For a man who knows so much about women," I said, "you've had your share of trouble with them."

I spent the rest of the day fitting a new stock to my shotgun, and just before supper time, Dale Buckley came around to see me. I went on working with the wood chisels and waited for him to start this conversation, figuring I'd take it up whichever way it went.

Buckley said, "I rode you pretty hard this morning, Page. I really didn't mean all the things I said."

"You meant them," I told him. "You had a right to say them."

He sighed. "Let's not discuss rights. Page, I'd give a thousand dollars to have a case in court tomorrow. Hell, you may be right but we'd have to prove it, and we just can't do it."

"Why the hell isn't Blake practicing medicine in town? He says he's not getting rich from the mine." I looked at him. "Is that so or is it a lie?"

"Well, according to the original assay of that location, there isn't a lot up there. Your dad and I checked it. Blake's making good wages, but hardly more." He scratched his cheek. "Somehow it does seem funny that he'd stick it out. Surely he could make five times that

81

much as a doctor in town."

"Then how come he don't?"

Buckley shrugged. "Maybe he likes the mountain air. Anyway, a man's reasons are his own."

"As long as they're good reasons," I said. "Dale, how do the bandits get rid of the gold?"

"We've never figured that out," Dale Buckley said. "I've spent several thousand dollars sending investigators to all the towns within three hundred miles, and none of them reported that an excess of gold bullion was deposited at any of the banks." He shook his head. "It's a matter that needs solving, Page. I can't give you an answer, but there certainly are some someplace, and mighty slick ones too. There's a good brain behind this whole operation." He started to turn away, then faced back. "Oh, what I came to tell you was that you don't have to appear in court tomorrow. Our attorney has advised us to drop the charges tonight."

CHAPTER 7

THERE WASN'T ANOTHER GOLD SHIPMENT SCHEDULED for three days, so I got in some loafing. Grandpa and I went hunting and I spent a day hanging around the stage office, waiting for Dale Buckley to thaw out. He didn't have much to say to me, and I suppose he had some grounds for acting like that; I'd put him in a spot, so to speak, and he wasn't forgetting it.

The only one who wasn't sore at me was Jim Bell. Now there was one swell guy; he understood me better than my own father did. Bell had to go into Rapid City and wanted me to go along with him, but I didn't think I ought to; I knew Buckley had a payload that he wanted to get out. But Bell spoke to Buckley about it and Dale put it off, so I rolled some blankets, picked up a saddle horse at the stable, and rode out of Deadwood with Jim Bell.

"Ma kind of likes you," Bell said, by way of breaking a long silence.

"Well, I like her," I said. "You ought to be proud of her, Jim."

"I am," Bell said. "You know, Page, I just naturally distrust a man who doesn't respect his mother. It's the way I was raised, I guess, but I've got no use for him if he doesn't respect his mother. Do you understand what I mean?"

"Sure. Well, no one can say that about you, Jim."

"I suppose that's right," Bell said. "As a matter of fact, I've been thinking of giving up my job and going someplace else."

"Where?"

He shrugged and rolled a cigarette, riding along with his reins dropped. "I haven't made up my mind to that. California, perhaps. We'll get a small place and work it. She hasn't many years left and I want them to be peaceful."

"When are you quitting?"

"Not right away. Six months, I guess. Before winter sets in." He looked at me and laughed. "Hell, I'm not in a hurry, Page. A man makes too many mistakes when he gets in a hurry."

We spent a night at Jake Spade's station, and I sat there until ten o'clock, watching Jim Bell play poker, then I got tired and went to bed. I guess it was around three when I woke up and went outside; the outhouses were near the barn. It was just one of those trips a man takes and doesn't make a lot of noise about it, and because of this I heard Jim Bell talking to someone in the dark doorway of the barn.

There was the barest sliver of a moon, not enough to really see by, yet I could distinguish the shapes standing there. I heard Bell say something softly, too softly to make out. Then the other man spoke and the sound of his voice made me pause; it was familiar to me, yet not so much so that I could readily recognize it.

So I stood there, and listened, but they spoke too softly, and I was just a few feet too far away to pick up the talk. The fact that Bell was there talking didn't arouse any suspicion at all; he talked to a lot of people. It was the other man's voice; I'd heard it before and I just couldn't place it. But I didn't associate it with anything pleasant.

A few minutes later the man with Bell stepped into the saddle. He turned as though to ride out, then paused and spoke in a clearer voice. "Will I see you in Deadwood, Jim?"

"It won't be necessary," Bell said.

I put the voice with the name then, Charles Blake, and watched him ride out, taking the Deadwood road. Since it wouldn't do to make my presence known, I waited until Jim Bell walked back to Jake Spade's station and went inside. Still I didn't follow him immediately.

A lot of possibilities ran through my mind. Charles Blake could have met Bell purely by accident, although I considered the chances of that mighty slim. Had Blake gone on into the station, I would have thought a lot less of it; that would have indicated that he was just passing through. But he hadn't been at the station when I went to bed, and he didn't stay long.

To me it just looked as though Blake knew that Bell would be here, and had come out for a talk. Which made a mighty strange thing of it, riding all that distance for five minutes of conversation.

I didn't see Bell when I went back inside; he was probably asleep or in his room. I couldn't go to sleep for thinking about it, and wondering what I should do about it. I thought I might just come right out and explain how it was I'd overheard the conversation, and then see what his reaction would be. But I decided against that. It might be better to play dumb and learn more about this before I made up my mind.

And I kept reminding myself that it wasn't Jim Bell I distrusted, but Dr. Charles Blake; the man had been a source of humiliation to me and I wasn't going to forgive him for it.

Jim Bell woke me in the morning; I was nearly late for breakfast, and afterward I saddled the horses and we rode on toward Rapid City. There must have been something in my manner or expression, for it made Bell curious.

Finally he said, "All right, suppose you tell me what it is, Page."

"Tell you what?"

"Whatever's bothering you," Bell said. "You're just not a moody man."

I was driven by curiosity and a desire to prove in my own mind Jim Bell's complete innocence, so I let my resolution slip away. "I was in the outhouse last night and saw you talking to Charles Blake."

Bell's eyes got sharp and his expression drew a little tight. "Oh? You've got sharp ears, huh?"

I shook my head. "No, I couldn't hear anything, except what Blake said just before he left. Jim, the man's a crook."

Bell studied me for a moment, then swore softly. I

didn't know how to make this out. Then he laughed. "God damn it, it looks like I've got to take you into my confidence whether I like it or not."

"I don't understand," I said.

"Of course you don't," Bell said, his manner again going relaxed and easy. "All right, Page, we might as well have it all; you'll peck at me now until you get it. Now I know you thought it strange as hell because I didn't want charges pressed against Blake or the Henry boys. Page, I just couldn't take action without upsetting the apple cart."

"You're not making sense to me."

"Let me put it this way. Some time ago I faced up to the fact that I wasn't going to crack the bandit gang by going around collecting evidence. I had to get a man on the inside, and Blake just fell into the job. He's doing right well at it too."

"For Pete's sake! An undercover man!"

"Yes, and you damned near pulled the cover off him," Bell said. "And at the worst possible time too. Blake was getting thick with the Henry brothers and they were just about to let him in on the gang leaders. But you broke that up."

"For gosh sakes, why didn't you belt me one?"

Jim Bell laughed. "To tell you the truth, I thought about it." Then he shook his head. "But I got to thinking that if I turned Blake and the Henry boys loose, no real damage would be done. That's what Blake rode out to see me about. He wanted me to know that he was going back to the mine and all had been forgiven."

I shook my head in amazement, and with a new understanding. "No wonder Dale and pa got so sore."

"They don't know anything about this," Jim Bell said. "And you're not going to tell them, do you understand?"

"Oh, sure. It's safe with me."

"It had better be or I'll skin you alive. And I mean that."

I knew he did, but he didn't have to worry. The day got brighter for me and I started grinning again. Then I said, "Blake must be boiling at me."

"He's not happy, but he'll get over it."

"Maybe if I went to him and—"

"You just leave him alone," Jim Bell said sharply. Then he smiled. "You understand, it'd be better if you didn't even speak to him."

"Sure," I said. "You don't have to worry about me, Jim."

"I know I don't," Ben said, and fell silent.

I never did find out what business Jim Bell had in Rapid City; he was pretty well set on taking care of it himself and I wanted to get a haircut and a barbershop shave. For my money we could have laid over the day, but Jim Bell wanted to start back and I let him have his way.

At the pace we traveled I knew we wouldn't make Spade's station in time for a decent night's sleep, so along toward evening I started looking for a likely campsite. Cutbanks flanked the stage road on both sides, and I knew there wasn't a handy creek for another three or four miles; it seemed like bad planning on Jim Bell's part.

The daylight began to fade rapidly, like it does in the mountains, and the gray smudge of coming night began to cut visibility sharply; in another ten minutes we'd groping our way along or just letting the horses find their own way.

When the first shot was fired from up ahead, it scared me so that I darned near jumped out of the saddle,

87

which probably saved my life. The rifle bullet caught the horse dead center in the forehead and he went down. Two other guns opened on us and I heard Bell's pistol slamming shots back. Then everything happened very fast and it was some time before I got them all straightened out.

My horse went down and as luck would have it, he rolled on the Purdy shotgun and broke the mechanism where the barrels joined the breech. So I couldn't fire a shot.

I saw Bell dash into the brush, still shooting, and the rifles kept popping away; I could hear the bullets thudding into my horse. To move at all would be asking for a bullet. I lay perfectly still, crouched against the horse, and I guess to the riflemen, in the poor light, it looked like they'd nailed me good.

Clearly I heard one man say, "Didn't you see him fall? Hell, he was dead when he hit the ground. "

Another said, "Then it won't hurt to look."

The first man was the arguing kind. "Hell, he didn't do any shooting back, did he? Let's go back to town."

I couldn't be exactly sure, but it sounded like Deke Henry's voice; I wasn't going to call out and ask. A moment later I heard horses on the road, riding anyway, and the coward in me made me wait another five minutes before moving

My first thought was to call to Jim Bell, but I thought better of it; the wrong people might hear me I didn't like the idea of standing in the middle of a lonesome stretch of road with night upon me and a damned lot of miles ahead to town.

Any minute now I expected Jim Bell to come back, but he didn't, so I started off down the road, hoping to make Jake Spade's station sometime after midnight. The livery stable saddle wasn't of much value but I carried it anyway; I left my broken shotgun there in the road.

Fortunately I never thought highly of cowboys and never wanted to be one, so I never wore their uncomfortable boots like Jim Bell did. Mine were the lace-up walking kind, so it really wasn't much of a stint to Jake Spade's station; I arrived there a little after two in the morning and headed for the door, since he still had some lamps lighted.

My hand went out for the latch and stopped.

Deke Henry said, "Go and get us another bottle, Mort."

I moved to the window and took a careful look inside. Mort Henry was getting up and crossing to Jake Spade's bar. Deke sat with his back to me and Clyde sat across from him, his concentration on the cards in his hand kept him from looking up and seeing me there.

Quickly I ducked down and went to the barn and without lighting a lantern I worked along the stalls until I found their horses. Like most men who carry a pistol, the Henry boys were in the habit of leaving their saddle guns in scabbards; I pulled all three rifles and sniffed the barrels and there was fresh black powder stink in all of them.

I guess legally it didn't prove a thing because a man can shoot at a lot of things, but to me it proved all I needed to prove. One by one, I went over the rifles, carefully ejecting the cartridges from the magazines to find out which held the most. Obviously none had reloaded, for the Spencer was nearly empty only two rounds remained. There was a '76 Winchester with eight rounds, but it was .44 and not up to the power I was used to; I figured that the Henry boys would jump behind tables as soon as I popped up and I needed a gun that would shoot through an inch of oak.

The third rifle was a .40-62, just what I wanted, and it held five rounds; the other three were probably in my horse. Standing there, with the rifle in my hands, I felt pretty big, like some righteous avenger about to swoop down on the guilty. But I got to thinking about it, about the things Jim Bell had told me, and it dampened my desire for revenge. The Henry boys were about to take Charles Blake into their confidence; a shooting now would likely set back Jim Bell's planning, or even ruin it.

So I put the blasted rifle back in the scabbard, climbed into the hay mow and went to sleep. I didn't even hear the Henry boys leave, but when I woke, which was well after sunup, they were gone.

Jake Spade seemed surprised to see me and remarked that he hadn't heard me ride in. I told him I'd walked and ordered a meal, putting it on the stage line's bill. I was on my second cup of coffee when a horseman rode up, flung off and came inside.

Jim Bell stared at me and said, "By God, I thought you were dead!"

"Where the hell did you go?" I asked.

He sat down across from me, took off his hat and wiped his forehead with a handkerchief. "I didn't hear that shotgun boom, and when I saw you go down, I figured they'd got you good." He turned to Spade, who was behind the bar. "Bring me a cup of coffee and put a slug of whiskey in it," Then he turned back to me. "I've been combing the country since daylight, but they got clean away."

"They won't be hard to find," I said evenly. "I recognized Deke Henry and his brothers. They spent the night here at Spade's, and I slept in the loft."

"That was a damned cool thing for them to do," Bell said. "And for you too."

I shrugged. "They left their rifles in the barn and I toyed with the idea of a shoot-out, but then I thought I'd better see you first. You know, Blake and all the work he's done."

"Good thinking," Bell said, his manner brightening. "By golly, there may be some hope for you yet. And I promise you, when it's time to put the rope around the Henry boys' necks, I'll let you do it."

CHAPTER 8

WHEN I GOT HOME, GRANDPA WAS PAINTING THE fence along the south side of the house. He had a bucket of calcimine and a big brush, and was working at an angry pitch; he was getting a good deal of it on the lawn and in ma's flower bed.

I stopped for a moment. "You get a new job, grandpa?"

"Punishment," he said. Then he turned and pointed the brush at me. "Your ma wants to see you." He grinned hugely. "I saved you the west side."

"How do you get into these messes?" I asked and went into the house. Mother was mixing something at the table and she stopped when I hung up my hat and coat.

"And where have you been?"

"I went over to Rapid City with Jim Bell." I walked over to the table to dip a finger in the mix and got my hand slapped for it. Nothing unusual there; I always got my hand slapped, and also a taste. But not such a good

91

taste this time.

"That's starch for your father's shirts, smart aleck."

"And that's just what it tasted like," I said. "Is there anything to eat?"

"It won't hurt you to wait until mealtime," she said. "Page, I'm not very happy with you, running off without telling me."

"There wasn't time," I said. "All right, the next time I'll tell you. What's grandpa in dutch for?"

"He disgraced himself." She pursed her lips as though just telling it was bad. "Last evening Dole Buckley paid him for his work. And he went to the saloon and got drunk. Your father had to go and get him." She went on mixing the starch, the spoon whipping furiously around the bowl. "Whatever gets into people to do those things?"

"It could be because you told him not to."

She stopped stirring and looked at me. "What does that mean? Now you explain that."

I shrugged. "I don't know as I can, ma. But I guess grandpa's like a kid; he's dependent on you and when you say he can't do a thing, he'll do it just to show you he can."

"That's ridiculous!"

"Yeah, I guess it is," I said and went to my room.

Ralph and Joe came home from school and woke me; they wanted some help in building rabbit hutches; Bert Simons who had a vegetable farm near the edge of town had given them a pair of biting, kicking jacks that he'd caught in a snare. So I spent the rest of the day with hammer and saw and chicken wire, and I had to loan them the money to buy that, which is kind of a lesson: when you help younger brothers, it costs you more than time.

After supper I sort of had an idea I'd stroll around and see how Emma Buckley was making out, but Dale beat me to it. He came to the house; I was sitting on the porch in my stocking feet, enjoying the evening coolness.

"Page, have you been up town since you got back?"

"No, I didn't even come in by the main street. Why?"

He sat on the porch railing. "Jim Bell told me of the waylay job. So it occurs to me that the bandits must think you're dead."

"Hardly a cheering thought."

"I've got a gold shipment ready to go. And a new shotgun for you. Say, twenty minutes?"

"All right."

Buckley stood up. "Catch the stage at the edge of town. The shotgun will be in the box. Curley's driving; he says the leg don't bother him that much." He took out a cigar and bit off the end, then left it unlighted in his mouth. "The bandits won't be looking for a shotgun guard tonight. Be on your toes, huh?"

"I like living enough to try," I said. He turned away, but stopped when I spoke again. "Dale, do you have an eight gauge sawed-off in the office?"

"No, but the blacksmith has a hacksaw and a file. I can make one in a hurry."

"Then do it. I'd like to carry a spare in the box, something easy to handle for close range."

"You could do in a buffalo at twenty yards with an eight gauge," Buckley said and went down the path.

When I went in to get my boots and coat, mother looked up from her sewing. Grandpa was sitting in the rocker, moving gently and acting as though he hated it. Mother said, "I suppose you're going somewhere?"

"Out with the stage," I said and left the house.

93

I picked a dark corner, one that I knew Curley would cut close on his turn out of town, and I waited, but not long. I heard him coming, and he slowed just enough for me to dash out, make a flying grab for the door, and climb up on top. I must have startled a woman passenger for she let out a surprised bleat, but some man inside assured her that this method of leaving town was not uncommon.

Curley grinned at me when I settled on the seat beside him.

"I thought you'd still be in bed," I said.

He shook his head. "The first three-four days wasn't bad, then the old woman got tired of waitin' on me." He banged his cast covered leg against the side of the foot box. "Couldn't hurt it if I tried." Then he reached down mad at times; these drivers always liked to demonstrate heavy artillery there."

"I'm looking for big game," I said and turned in the seat to take a look at the luggage rack. It was fairly crowded by canvas satchels, but there was room enough for me to lay belly flat and be completely hidden from anyone who waited up ahead on the road.

When I started to climb back, Curley said, "My company that bad?"

"You'll look better alone tonight," I said.

The long barreled ten gauge I cradled against me, where I could get it into action instantly, but the sawed-off I wedged in between some satchels; that was my ace-in-the-hole in case I needed it.

I had no idea how much we were carrying, but I figured it was plenty for the stage was heavy; there was at least a hundred pounds of dust in the box, and probably six hundred pounds of samples in the boot, going to another assayer for a double check. Miners were always a distrustful lot.

Sixty-five thousand would be a fair guess, and it was close enough to make me a little nervous. There wasn't a shred of doubt in my mind that the bandits knew the stage was heavy tonight, or that they'd hit it, especially since they thought it was without a guard. I wondered if my presence was Dale Buckley's private secret, or had he let my father and Jim Bell in on it.

Curley drove as he always drove, daringly, fast, a little mad at times; these drivers always liked to demonstrate their great skill, and it took just that to handle six horses. Now and then he'd wheel around a corner close enough to scrape the hub; I'd feel the coach lurch slightly and I could understand why the blacksmith was always cussing out the drivers for eating up hub bearings. A couple of corners and they'd have so much dirt mixed with the grease that they had a grinding compound rather than a lubricant.

I kept an eye on the terrain, and the road ahead, what I could see of it. There was no telling where the action would take place; I figured I could only be on the lookout for it.

The log across the road was something neither I nor Curley expected and he barely had time to halt the team. I could see the two men on the other side, and Curley threw up his hands, then flung himself to the floor of the box when I yelled, "DOWN!"

They hadn't seen me; I was a complete surprise to them. I butted the Greener to my shoulder and swept a man completely off his feet, but I ended up in more trouble than I'd counted on. Being used to the Purdy tapped me up; I was accustomed to having some room between the triggers, so when I touched off the front trigger of the Greener, the damned thing went back, caught my other finger and let go both barrels.

And of course the recoil knocked me flat and nearly broke my shoulder. I went down in a tumble of satchels as one of the bandits shouted: "That was both barrels! Get him!"

I fumbled for the sawed-off, swung it just as a man charged the coach from the side of the road. He got a good charge in the leg for he went down and rolled, then dragged himself into the brush. I could have killed him then and there, but there just wasn't any sense to it.

The third bandit started for cover and I suppose I could have loaded him down a little, but I let him go. Curley raised his head and said, "Is it all over, kid?"

"Looks like."

I got down and he followed me, taking a lantern along. Some distance away we could hear horses moving out, and a man's loud cursing. The passengers started to get out of the coach, but I motioned them back. "Just stay in the coach, please. We'll take care of this."

The dead man was behind the fallen tree and while Curley held the lantern, I reached down and ripped off his mask. Deke Henry looked as ornery dead as he ever had alive.

Curley said, "Do you suppose the other two were Clyde and Mort?"

"That could be," I said and looked at the log across the road. "How the hell do we clear that away?"

"There's some rope in the coach. You get it and I'll unhitch two of the horses."

To say that we made short work of it wouldn't be the truth; it took us a good thirty-five minutes to clear the road. After Curley finished hitching the team, I said, "I'm going to let you go on in alone, Curley."

96

"Mr. Buckley ain't going to like that, kid."

"Well, he'll have to be mad then. The last time I stopped a bandit, they carted him away. This time I'd like to see that it doesn't happen. Or if it does, I want to know who came and got him."

"You mean, you're going to stay here?"

"What else?"

Curley scratched his head. "There's considerable downgrade between here and Jake Spade's place. Suppose you take two horses, one to ride, and the other to pack Deke on, and head back for Deadwood? We'll find something to wrap him in."

"That's going to slow you down, just four horses."

"Well, I don't maintain much of a schedule anyway."

Getting Deke wrapped and tied to a horse who was shying at the smell of blood wasted some more time, but finally I went one way and the stage the other. After it pulled out of sight, I got to thinking that if it was held up now, I might as well get clean out of the country; Dale Buckley would be after my scalp.

It was quite early in the pre-dawn hours when I stopped at the jail and kicked on the door until Jim Bell got up and answered it. He squinted at me, then said, "What the hell is it, Page?"

"Got a present for you," I said, jerking a thumb toward Deke Henry, face down across the horse. Bell cursed softly and had a look, then took me by the arm and led me inside. He lit a lamp before saying anything.

"Tell me about it."

"I was riding shotgun tonight."

His eyes widened. "I didn't see you leave."

"Buckley's idea. I got on at the edge of town."

He actually seemed displeased for a moment, then he said, "God damn it, why wasn't I notified about this?

97

I'm the law, ain't I?" He ran his fingers through his rumpled hair. "By golly, I'm going to say a thing or two to Buckley about this. Was Deke alone?"

I held up three fingers. "Someone is carrying buckshot in the legs. Maybe you'd better check with Charles Blake."

"I know how to do my job," Bell said.

This touchiness I put down to being rousted out of bed at such an odd hour. I turned to the door. "All right, I'm not bothering you, Jim. Anyway, they'll probably take the man to Blake to get the buckshot removed. Likely he'll get in touch with you about it tomorrow."

"Likely," Bell said and I went out.

Something told me I'd better see Dale Buckley right away, so I went to his place. Standing on the porch I could smell the fresh paint; he'd had it done over to make it a little nicer for his sister. I banged on the door, then someone came down the stairs with a lamp. When the front curtain parted, I saw Emma standing there.

"It's Page Sheridan. I've got to talk to your brother, Emma."

She slid the bolt and opened the door. "You frightened me," she said. "I'll call him."

But she didn't have to, Dale came down the stairs carrying a pistol. When he saw me he laid it on a hall table.

"What are you doing back in town?"

"We got held up."

His complexion blanched. "Good God, you didn't lose the gold, did you?"

I shook my head. "Curley went on with it." Then I glanced at Emma. "There's no need for you to be up."

"Did you shoot another man?" she asked.

"Yes."

"That doesn't sound as horrible as it once did," she said. "What happened?"

I told it quickly and they listened, then Dale Buckley said, "I'm going to see Bell in the morning and find out why we can't locate the wounded man. This is the first genuine lead we've had. If the injured man is one of the Henry boys, then we'll arrest the other and sweat him until he talks."

It was in my mind to tell Dale Buckley about Charles Blake, but I figured it would be a foolish thing to do. Now that things had gone this way, Jim Bell would probably do it himself, and it wasn't worth it to me to pass out the information and get the reputation of a blabbermouth.

Emma said, "Come in the kitchen and I'll make some coffee."

"That's a good idea," Buckley said and took my arm. "I don't know whether to be sore or not, you letting Curley go on alone. But I suppose if you hadn't, they'd have come back for Deke Henry."

"That's the way I figured it. I didn't want it to be another grave somewhere in the hills."

"Yes, we need a corpse." Buckley said. He sat down at the table. "Page, you're running a lot of risks. It isn't easy for me to set a man up as a target. And that's what you're turning into. The bandits are going to have to get rid of you or the operation's going to get too costly. That's why it's important to work fast, get them in jail or at the end of a rope before your luck runs out."

"Somehow or another," I said, "you always manage to brighten my day." I smiled, but there wasn't anything to smile about; he'd spoken the truth.

CHAPTER 9

THERE WAS NO SENSE IN MY KEEPING DALE BUCKLEY up so I went home. I don't think anyone could have entered the house more quietly than I, but grandpa heard me and came into my room just as I was unlacing my boots.

"Thought you was on the road," he said.

"I was," I said, then told him about the attempted holdup. He squatted there on the floor and listened carefully, and I took him into my confidence concerning the matter Jim Bell and I had discussed, and that affair east of Spade's station.

When I finished, grandpa said, "Why, I never heard such pap."

"What do you mean, grandpa?"

"You've been took in, son."

I shook my head. "Not by Jim Bell. I'd trust him with my life."

"Maybe you should and maybe you shouldn't. But you're a fool to buy a man's story without lookin' into it."

"Aw, now don't get suspicious," I said. "Besides, Jim told me to keep my nose out of his business."

He chuckled without humor. "Son, when a man's shot at, anything is his business that'll clear it up." He tabbed off the points with his fingers. "Ain't it a mite strange to you for Buckley and Bell to pass off as nothin' the capture of that doctor and his friends?"

"Jim Bell explained that, grandpa."

"He gave you a mouthful of words," grandpa said. "As far as I'm concerned, either of 'em could be givin' information to the outlaws."

"Grandpa, dad could be too. Don't you suspect him?"

"Hell, I know Fred," he said. "He's too strait-laced and honest to even think of it."

"And so's Jim Bell and Dale Buckley," I pointed out.

"That's yet to be proved," he said. "For my part, I've been cooped up here for days now, and it's time to get out and smell the wind. You want to come along?"

"To where?"

"Blake's mine."

"Now grandpa—"

"I guess I can go it alone then," he said and got up.

Of course it was silly to be afraid for him, but I was. "All right, I'll go too. But can we please just look and not get Jim Bell sore?"

"Why, that was my only intention, just to look."

I laced up my boots again and picked up the sawed-off shotgun; I was through for life with a Greener; a weapon was either clumsy or not, and if it was, a man was wasting his time perfecting a skill to overcome some inherent weakness built into the gun.

We left the house quietly and walked to the stables behind the stage office. Hal Butram was the night hostler and we woke him; he was a man with a grumbly disposition, but he got us two horses and we left town.

When grandpa was on the move, he wasn't much for talk, and as well as I knew the country, I had to admit that he knew it a lot better, not from having been over it before, but from an accumulation of years of traveling. He knew the way land went, how the rises peaked out, and there was no twisting him around as to direction, no losing him once he'd set a path in his mind. And he had the ability to remember where he'd been; every landmark stood out in vivid detail in his mind as though he drew a mental map as he went along.

We moved along without raising a noise, and an hour or so before dawn we came out of the brush near Charles Blake's mine. I had expected to see a lamp burning inside, and there was one. Grandpa and I dismounted and tied our horses some distance from the cabin.

"He likes late hours," grandpa said.

"One of the Henry boys is in there, badly shot up," I said.

"Is that a fact?"

"I told you Blake was working for Jim Bell." My impatience with him was evident. "Hell, how else could he gain the confidence of the bandits if he didn't—"

"That story is makin' my ears tired," grandpa said flatly.

I didn't think he had any reason for getting short with me; I got short right back. "Now that you've had your look, are you satisfied?"

"I ain't had it yet," grandpa said and moved toward the cabin.

We gained the wall by the window, and none too soon for Mort Henry came out. He left the door open and Charles Blake followed him, he closed the door, and the two men stood there a moment in the darkness.

Then Blake said, "I'm going to have to take the leg off, Mort."

"Sonofabitch," Mort Henry said.

"It's the kneecap. I just can't save the knee at all."

"Sonofabitch."

"Is that all you can say, sonofabitch?" Blake asked. "If you hadn't bungled the damned job in the first place, Clyde wouldn't be in that fix." He took a cigar from his pocket and lit it. "You'd better tell Reno to get some men up here. I've got a shipment to get out. Hell, everything's come to a standstill since Buckley hired that damned kid."

"Hell, it ain't all my fault. Teel Reno was supposed to work him over in the alley, but they bungled that." He shuffled his feet. "Our luck's going bad, doc."

"Nonsense," Blake snapped. "And send Reno and a few others back here. I can't leave Clyde now. Not even for an hour." Mort Henry stood there a moment longer, then nodded. Blake took him by the arm. "And you find out why the devil the information on this last stage wasn't right."

"All right," Henry said and went to the leanto for his horse.

Blake watched him ride out, then went back inside the cabin.

Grandpa inclined his head and we moved away from the wall. With some stunted brush screening us from the house we talked it over. "I gather he's talkin' about stolen gold," grandpa said. He scratched his whiskers. "Probably in the mine shaft right now."

"I wonder where he takes the stuff," I said. "Not to Rapid City. People would know about it."

"How?"

"Gold has characteristics, grandpa. Any good assayer who knew the country could tell which vein it came from unless it had been smelted and put into bars. And none of this gold is. After the ore leaves the crusher it's amalgamated. At the smelter it needs further refining."

"I expect you got that out of a book."

"I learned it from pa," I said. "Grandpa, you want to take a look inside the mine?"

"Hoped you'd say that." He looked at the sky. "Maybe an hour left before dawn. Why not?"

We shifted around the outbuildings and went inside

the shaft, bending low to keep from bumping our heads. Blake had tunneled back a way and stoped it well, and he'd dug a few finger tunnels to the right. Grandpa went on ahead; I couldn't see a thing. He couldn't either but he had picked up a stick and was using it as a blind man would; he didn't stumble over anything.

I was surprised when we found the stolen gold, four sacks of it, but after thinking about it, I guess it had been about as good a place as any. A man guarded his own mine and there was no chance of anyone getting inside for a look, unless they had a reason like we did. Anyone else wasn't going to risk getting shot for a look into what everyone knew was a poor vein.

Grandpa found a miner's lamp and lit it. I said, "What are you going to do?"

"Steal some gold," grandpa said. He pointed to some sacks. "We'll put the gold in them and fill these sacks with dirt."

I thought it was such a good idea that I grabbed one of the sacks and he hit me across the arm. "Put that down, you damned fool!" He picked up the miner's lamp and examined the puckered mouth of each sack. "Just as I thought. There's a horsehair stuck in wax around each one. Sonny, you're not dealing with stupid or careless people. Try and remember that."

"You don't have to bawl me out," I said, my feelings a little hurt.

Transferring the gold was more of a job than I thought; it took us nearly twenty-five minutes, but we got the job done, and done to grandpa's horse-thief instincts, you'd never have known the sacks had been touched. He remelted the wax with the miner's lamp, resprinkled the dust back on the sacks and placed them exactly as they had been, even turning them just so, in case that was a check of Charles Blake's.

In all I guess we had a hundred and eighty pounds. We left the mine, paused at the mouth for a look around, then got out of there and to our horses. With dawn just over the horizon, it wasn't safe to take the road so grandpa led out and we started across country, through some of the most outlandishly rough terrain I'd ever been through.

Again, a blanket of silence fell over grandpa, and it wasn't until we stopped at Willow Creek to water the horses that he spoke. "Now that we got the gold, let's light out for California, get us some young women and live it up."

"You're joking."

"Well, only half way," he said. "I'm too honest to deny the temptation." He bit off a chew of tobacco. "You going to give this to Buckley?"

"Sure."

"Better give it to your dad."

I frowned. "Now you're not going to start that again, are you?"

He shrugged. "Your dad's too dumb to be dishonest."

"By God, that's not very nice!"

"Well, I don't always say nice things," he told me and got on his horse.

I thought it was best to stay clear of the town, and we took a roundabout way to the mine, tying up before the office building. I shouldered my share and we went in. Father was in his office and he frowned when I pushed the door open with my foot. And his desk groaned a little when we put the sacks on it.

"What's this?" he asked.

"Gold. We think it's yours." I enjoyed saying that, enjoyed the expression on his face. He got up and went to the door and shouted down the hall for Rudy Butler, the company assayer.

Butler came in, hurrying; few men tarried when my father got that tone in his voice. Father said, "Rudy, run tests on each sack. Page says it's our gold."

Rudy Butler took some manila envelopes from his frock pocket and filled each one. Then he went back to his laboratory. My father sat down and gnawed on his cigar. "Now start from the beginning and make sense."

"We went to Blake's place again," I said.

"After Jim Bell told you not to?"

"Bell don't run me," I said. "Mort and Clyde Henry were there. Clyde's going to lose his leg; that buckshot charge got him bad."

"Tell me about the gold."

"We overheard Blake tell Mort that he had a shipment to go out. That could only mean the gold from the last robbery. So we took a look inside his shaft and found these bags. Actually they were in other sacks, but we transferred the stuff and filled his sacks with dirt."

He stared at us for a minute, then roared with laughter.

Grandpa said, "I don't think it's funny."

Father calmed himself. "I'm not laughing at you. It's just that Blake is going to be surprised as hell when he gets rid of that gold and discovers it's low grade ore from his own mine." He wiped the tears from his eyes. "Page, go get Bell and Buckley. I'm going to swear out a warrant against Blake."

"That wouldn't be smart," grandpa said mildly.

"Now I didn't ask you," father said.

"That's so, but it don't change anything. Blake ain't the big auger. He's high up, but he ain't the top man. That fish story Bell told the boy don't set well with me.

And Buckley ain't what I'd say was clean enough either."

"Why, you old fool, Buckley's honest as the day is long!"

"I don't know that. You don't either. He's only said so."

Father sighed and wiped a hand across his face. "I suppose it wouldn't hurt to keep this to ourselves, at least until Blake discovers the switch. Then we'll see who acts, and how." He smoked his cigar and gave this some thought. "I've always wondered why Blake hung onto that mine; it's not rich enough to pay more than day wages, working it by hand. Of course a big company could make it pay with machinery, but Blake won't sell. I know because we've tried to buy it."

"There's no doubt that Blake is using his mine as a cover for his gold. But you checked in Rapid City and Blake's never brought in enough to the smelter to make anyone suspicious. And we have to rule out his spreading the gold thinly; they've stolen too much to do that."

He got up and walked to a wall map. "There's a smelter going in Custer and one in Belle Fourche. I think it would be a smart thing if I went to Judge Wayne and got a court order to have their records examined by the marshal." He looked at his watch. "The judge ought to be through pruning his roses by now. I'll take care of that, Page. You get some sleep. We'll leave on the four o'clock stage."

"What about me?" grandpa asked.

"Dawn wants you to spade the rutabaga patch."

"I won't do it," grandpa said.

Father faced him. "Do you want weak coffee, burned eggs for a week?" He took grandpa by the arm and shook him gently. "Use your head, man. Don't fight a woman when she wants her way."

"I'm my own boss," grandpa said. "I'll spade the garden when I put a mind to it."

"She wants it done this afternoon," father said. "I'd do it."

"Then do it," grandpa said and went out.

After he'd gone, father said, "He's not easy to get along with, but I suppose you wouldn't agree with that."

"I guess I wouldn't," I said and went back to town.

Jim Bell was crossing the street as I passed through and he couldn't help seeing me; he waved me over to the hitchrack and smiled. "I went over to your house fifteen minutes ago and your mother told me you hadn't been home."

"I had some runnin' around to do."

Bell looked at my horse and saw that he was tired. "I guess you did."

"What did you want, Jim?"

"I had a statement for you to sign," Bell said. "The judge wanted it for the records. You just don't kill a man and not give the details."

"The judge is getting a little fussy, isn't he? He didn't want any—"

"Well, I didn't intend to argue about it," Bell said. "Why don't you come over to my office and do it now?"

He had a tone there that told me I ought to do it or he was going to get nasty about it, so I wheeled my horse and made my way through the traffic and dismounted in front of his office. He opened the door and stood aside so I could go in.

Then he unbuckled his gunbelt and rolled it around the holster before placing it on his desk. "Page," he said, "I get the feeling that you don't always tell me the truth."

"For instance."

"Well, like where you were all night."

It was a shock to know that he didn't trust me, after I'd trusted him. "With a girl," I said.

His expression got a little flat and his eyes grew sharper. "Don't get smart with me, Page."

"All right, I'll get stupid then. Can I go now?"

He studied me, tried to break me down by just staring at me, but I didn't crumble. Finally he spun a paper around on his desk and edged a pen toward me. I read it carefully and signed it.

Jim Bell said, "You worry me, Page. I just know that you're going to knock my best plans into a cocked hat."

"We've all got to worry about something," I said and went on home.

Grandpa was spading the rutabaga patch and mother was gossiping across the back fence; when she saw me go in the back door she broke off the conversation and came in. I was splashing water on my face and she said, "Where have you been?"

"Is that all anyone can ask me?" I started to reach for the towel but she jerked it out of reach and slapped a washrag in my hand.

"Not until you get all the dirt off. Dale Buckley has been here twice this morning. He's irritated that you went off without telling him about it. If you're not careful, you'll get fired, and it'll serve you right."

"I thought you didn't want me to have the job."

"It's a disgrace to be fired," she said, and went back to her talk.

CHAPTER 10

ALTHOUGH I WAS BONE WEARY, MY MIND JUST wouldn't let my body rest in peace, and I lay on my bed, thinking about a lot of things. And the more I thought, the more suspicious I became. I was sure of one thing: I no longer trusted Jim Bell. And I was unsure of another thing: whether I trusted Dale Buckley or not.

Finally I got up and sat at my writing desk, composing three short notes. Two of them weren't hard to write, but the third one was. And I printed all three of them, disguising my handwriting so that it wouldn't be recognized.

I went downstairs and my mother looked around the kitchen door. "Where are you going now?"

"Uptown for a little while." I went out without explaining further, knowing full well that she was vexed by short answers. My two brothers came storming down the street, hit me up for a dime apiece, then ran on home to discuss how to spend it.

I stopped at the hotel first. Ronny Searle was at the desk and he had a lot to talk about. Somehow, I always felt a little sorry for Ronny; he wanted so to be a participant in life and always found himself in the role of fearless spectator. It wasn't difficult to slip one of the notes into Dale Buckley's box without being seen; nearly everyone in town picked up their mail at the hotel, and I knew that Buckley would get the message by supper time.

Getting Jim Bell's note to him was more difficult; I had to observe the jail for some time before I saw him leave, and then I had to be careful not to be noticed as I slipped the note under his door.

With the second message out of the way, I walked on down the street to the post office. It wasn't easy for me to put the third message in an envelope and address it, but I felt that I had to do it; I had to be certain beyond all doubt, logically sure, without a tinting of emotion. I dropped the letter into the slot and went on home to wait for my father.

I was sleeping in a chair on the front porch when he came home; he slapped me on the leg with a court order, then said, "We've got forty minutes until stage time. Better eat something; you won't get anything until morning."

As he passed by me I noticed that he'd picked up the mail and I felt a little sick at the stomach. But not too sick to go into the kitchen and make a cold meat sandwich. While I was eating; I heard a bellow from the parlor and rushed in. Father was standing there, swearing.

He thrust a letter at me "Read this garbage! By God these cranks ought to be prosecuted to the fullest extent of the law! And if there's no law against it, there ought to be one!"

It wasn't easy to read my own printing, and yet it was the easiest thing I ever did, for I had no doubts now.

BANDIT LEADER:
I KNOW YOU ARE GIVING INFORMATION AS TO WHEN GOLD IS SHIPPED. MEET ME AT TEN O'CLOCK SATURDAY NIGHT AT THE OLD REEDER MINE.
ONE WHO KNOWS ALL

Father snatched the letter from my hand. "By George, I'm going to the authorities with this!"

"What good will it do?"

"I don't know, but it can't hurt anything." He was as angry as I'd ever seen him, and I wanted to tell him the whole truth, but I was afraid to; he would think that I distrusted him, and perhaps I did, in a way, or I wouldn't have been able to write the note in the first place.

He was determined to do something; he snatched up his hat and stalked to the door, and I tagged along. As we stepped onto the front porch. Dale Buckley came up the walk, and he was in a bad humor. He also waved his note angrily.

"Fred, this is the damnedest outrage!"

"You too?" father asked.

Buckley calmed down; I don't believe he felt as picked on.

"Did you get one, Fred?" They exchanged notes. "The same," Dale said. "I don't understand it."

"I can explain it," I said.

Father said, "You keep out of this." Then he turned and looked at me. "What did you say?"

"I said that I could explain it, sir."

"You'd damned better and if I don't like it, I'll blister your hide."

I wanted them to sit down, but they wanted to stand,. and they looked at me as though I were fascinating. "Well," I said, "it's for sure that someone is giving out information on shipments. It could be you, Dale, or you, pa."

"So?" father said, in a tone I didn't like. "I know Dale didn't, and he knows I didn't."

"No, sir, you really didn't know. You thought you knew, but it wasn't proof."

"Then I suppose this foul hoax is," Buckley snapped.

"I think it is. Dad, if you'd been the one, what would

112

you have done when you read the note?"

"Well, I danged sure wouldn't have spouted off and—" He stopped and he was no longer angry. "I see what you mean. Do you see, Dale?"

"Yes. Page, how many of these did you write?"

"One more. I slipped it under Jim Bell's door."

Father nodded to the chairs and they sat down; I leaned against the porch post. "Suppose Bell does nothing? How will we know?"

"If Jim's the one, he'll be at the old mine on time," I said.

"You know," Dale Buckley said, "it just may work. Page, I think you've got something here." He looked at father. "I vote to give Page a free hand."

"There's a great deal of danger connected with this," father said.

"No more than sitting up on that stage box," I said.

"He's got a good point there, Fred. Hell, he can take care of himself. He's proved that." He leaned forward. "Look, why don't you get on the stage as you planned? Page can get off at the Spanish Flat station and come back tomorrow night in time to meet Bell, or whoever it is. I'll go talk to Bell, sound him out. If he lets on to me that he's gotten his note, I'll contact Page so he won't have to wait after that. It could be that we're way wrong here, and it's not Bell at all."

"Who then?" I asked. "Only three people know when there'll be gold shipped."

"Plus the men who load it," Dale said.

"Not in the last ninety days," father said. "Half the time they've been loading sand. If someone at the mine was tipping off the bandits, they'd know what was sand and what wasn't." He smiled. "Deke Henry got himself killed over twelve sacks of sand."

113

"I never knew that," Dale Buckley said. "Fred, I accepted that shipment, insured it, in good faith."

"That's right. And it positively proves to me that no one at the mine is tipping off the bandits, or they'd have passed it up, knowing it was sand. But you didn't know, and neither did Jim Bell, so the leak was between two men. Now we know it wasn't you, Dale. As a clincher, you put Page on the stage as it left town to surprise the bandits. You wouldn't have done that if you'd been the contact man for the gang."

"Well," Buckley said, smiling, "it's good to have a clean slate." Then he frowned. "I guess we've got a case against Jim Bell."

"Yes," father said. "But we'll clinch it tomorrow night. Page, be careful. Bell would kill you in a minute if he thought—"

"I'll have him covered," I said, "because grandpa's going with me."

"It might be best, for your mother's sake, to keep him out of it."

I shook my head in disagreement. "He's got Indian in him, and if any man covers my back, it'll be grandpa."

"Fred, it's his neck. Don't you think he ought to decide how he'll work it?"

"I guess," father said. He glanced at his watch. "Stage time. Let's get on with this."

As we walked to the station, I said, "Are you still going to check the records at the smelter?"

"I'd be a fool if I didn't," father said. "I've got to know how Blake disposes the gold and where. Page, I want the whole gang."

The stage was made up and waiting when we arrived; we got aboard immediately and I took the backward riding seat and was asleep before we were a mile from

114

town. Father woke me when we stopped at the Spanish Flats station; the other passengers were going inside.

Father said, "It's a quarter to eight. You ought to be back in Deadwood by eleven-thirty." He handed me a key. "This will let you into my office. Sleep there. Grandpa will join you there tomorrow night; and be careful, both of you."

"You don't have to worry, pa."

"I do worry, because I am your pa." He slapped me on the shoulder. "I'll send the hostler out. Leave quietly. I don't think you'll attract any attention."

"When will you be back to town?"

He thought a moment. "If I don't find anything in Custer, I'm going on to Belle Fourche. Three days on the outside. Sooner, if I turn up anything at the smelter in Custer."

He got out of the coach. "Stay here, and give me ten minutes to send the hostler out."

I sat in the coach and finally when I saw the hostler leave the station and go to the barn, I got out and followed him. He was putting a saddle on a rangy bay and he looked at me as though he could see a price tag on my head. I didn't explain myself or thank him, just mounted up and rode out. I was only twenty-five or so miles from Deadwood, but I didn't waste a lot of time getting there. Going to the mine without being seen was no problem; the main building was dark when I let myself in and I didn't light a lamp. There was a storeroom next to father's office and I bedded down there and went to sleep.

I spent a mighty boring Saturday, for I had to remain quiet; the assayer and some other men worked in the building until six o'clock. To amuse myself I read one of father's books on hydraulic mining, certainly educational, but hardly light reading. Finally the assayer and the others went home and the building grew dark. I waited awhile, then went out and unlocked the front door so grandpa could get in; there was something I wanted to ask him anyway.

He was the kind of a man you never hear coming up; he was just there in the darkness, not ten feet away.

"Been waitin' long, son?"

He stepped inside and I closed the door. "Tell me, grandpa, how did you know I'd be here? How did pa know you'd come here?"

He chuckled in that irritating way he had. "You're blind in one eye and can't see out of the other, son. Hell, all the time you was sittin' on the porch, gabbin', I was squattin' in the flower bed alongside the house listenin'. That's the kind of work your ma figures I'm fit fer, weedin' flowers."

"Yes, but—"

"Son, I ain't stupid. When you came back, you couldn't go home, and you couldn't go to the hotel. I could guess that and your pa knew it." He handed me a package. "Here's some grub. I know you ain't had any."

He'd thought of everything, and I sat down to eat the ham and cold potatoes. Grandpa said, "You figure Bell will come?"

"Why not? It's got to be Bell."

"Hard for me to believe. I liked the man."

"You think I didn't?"

He scratched his whiskers. "Be hard on his ma. She thinks the sun rises and sets in him."

"I can't be responsible for that, grandpa, but I'm sorry for her."

Grandpa sighed. "How you goin' to work it?"

"I thought I'd wait inside the mine," I said. "You can

find some high ground and cover my back."

"Then stay out of that mine," grandpa said. "Was I Bell, that's where I'd put my men. Now, get high and look down on your game, son. Safer that way, and you'll need all you can get, because if Bell's the man, he'll be dangerous."

"Yeah. Let's get started, huh?"

It was only two miles to the old mine, so we went afoot. Grandpa picked out the spot for me, a nest of rocks in a position where I faced the mine shaft squarely, still within easy range of my sawed-off shotgun. And then Grandpa took off to find his own spot, and I couldn't tell where he was, except that I knew his position would be good. We were in a long, shallow canyon, open at both ends; I had no idea which direction Bell would come from, or how many men he had with him.

It certainly was a crawly feeling, sitting there, waiting, and thinking that maybe they were already in the rocks behind you, just waiting for some signal to blast you to eternity. And certainly Jim Bell wouldn't come clumping into the canyon making a lot of noise. If he showed up it would only be for one thing, to kill the man who'd written the note and shut his mouth forever. No, he'd come in without a sound, and wait for me to make the mistake. I couldn't allow that.

The night was dark, yet a man's eyes grew accustomed to it and I was able to pick out rock outcroppings and the turn of the canyon and the black maw of the mine. Keeping track of time was a problem, because three minutes seemed like thirty, and I got pretty well mixed up on it. So it was natural for me to overwait the whole thing; I hadn't intended on doing that at all, but it happened.

117

It was well after ten, almost ten-thirty when I detected a slight movement down the canyon; a man was approaching on foot and doing a quiet job of it. I held the triggers back on my shotgun and cocked both hammers, holding them while I released the triggers so they'd catch the sears; that way there was no metallic click to give me away.

I let him come on, then I said, "All right, Jim, that's far enough!"

He jumped at the sound of my voice; the canyon bounced it around and he couldn't place it as to position. That grandpa was pretty smart at that.

"Drop your guns, Jim! I won't tell you again!"

I heard a pistol fall, then Bell said, "Page, is that you? You damned fool, what are you trying to do?"

"Put your hands up and keep them there," I warned and vacated my place in the rocks. It was a mistake; I knew it as soon as my feet touched the canyon floor for a shotgun boomed from the mouth of the mine shaft and a pellet nicked my arm; the rest of the charge splattered against rock. I saw Jim Bell make a dive for his fallen pistol, and I yelled at him: "Don't do it, Jim!"

But he wasn't listening, or he didn't care, or maybe he thought he could beat me. He didn't beat me. I cut him down just as he raised the gun and then the hidden shotgun man in the mine shaft made a dash for it and made the rocks before I could get off a shot. It couldn't have done any good anyway for he was out of the sawed-offs range.

Grandpa came charging down the canyon and I cautiously approached Jim Bell. He was still alive, twisting in pain on the ground and I kicked the fallen pistol out of his reach.

CHAPTER 11

GRANDPA SCOUTED UP SOME BRUSH, KICKED IT INTO A pile near Jim Bell, and lit it; then I could see that I'd wounded him badly in the side near his belt line. Bell's face was drawn into a grimace, and he breathed hard, painfully.

"Jim," I said, "why did you do it? I told you not to go for your gun."

"Wouldn't have shot—at you—kid. Ambush—in the tunnel."

That didn't make sense to me, but I couldn't jaw about it while he bled to death. "Grandpa, find his horse and get to town and bring one of the doctors back. Even if you have to do it at gunpoint."

"We'll do her," grandpa said and started off.

I did the best I could for Jim Bell, putting a compress on the wound and making him as comfortable as possible, and it seemed like a very long time before the doctor returned. I don't think grandpa had had to use his gun, but from the doctor's expression I knew he'd been threatened; you can always tell because they resent the threat more than what they have to do.

It was the little Frenchman, DuJoir. He looked at Bell, then said, "Get him in my buggy. I've got to take this man in immediately."

We had to hurt Jim Bell to move him, but you couldn't consider a detail like that when a man's life was at stake. I didn't want to see him die, guilty or not. And that was pure coward talking; it wasn't going to be me that killed him. Hang him if they wanted, but I'd done too much already.

When we got back to town, I paced up and down the

119

doctor's parlor; he was behind closed doors with his nurse, and I guess he was having a busy time of it. Grandpa sat in a chair near the wall; he seemed glum and uncommunicative. Finally he said, "Did you recognize the jasper hidin' in the mine?"

"No. It was too dark, and I was concentrating on Jim Bell."

"He got out in a big hurry," Grandpa said. "Not much on fight, was he?"

The front door opened and Mrs. Dance came in; she looked at Grandpa, then at me, and said, "When he didn't come back like he said he would, I knew something had happened." She folded and unfolded her hands. "Then a fella come to the house and said he'd seen my Jim bein' brought into town, bad hurt."

I moved a chair around for her. "Mrs. Dance, won't you please sit down?"

"He ain't dead is he?"

"No, he's—well, the doctor's working on him." I pulled a chair around and faced her. "Mrs. Dance, what did Jim tell you? Did he say where he was going?"

"He don't worry me much with his work," she said. "But he did say that he had to do somethin' important." She looked steadily at me. "Was you with my Jim when it happened?"

I nodded, then said, "Mrs. Dance, I shot him."

"It was an accident?"

"No, he was going for his gun after I told him not to." I just couldn't sit there and have her look at me, without blame or anything in her eyes. I got up and began to pace back and forth again.

"Jim wouldn't do a harm to you," she said. "Why, he liked you as good as any man he knew."

I hated to hurt her, but I had to. "Mrs. Dance, we have

120

every reason to believe that Jim's the leader of the bandits."

Her mouth drew into a firm line. "My Jim a thief? That's a lie!"

"I wish it were a lie," I said.

"Well, it *is* a lie. Jim wouldn't steal. He doesn't have to."

"A mother's loyalty—"

She stamped her foot to silence me. "I'm not talking about loyalty. I'm talking about what a man is inside. He ain't twisted. He stands straight. And a straight man don't steal."

The front door opened and Dale Buckley came in. "Page, I heard you shot—" Then he saw Mrs. Dance sitting there and his manner softened. "I'm sorry, madam. Very sorry."

"You're not sorry," she said. "You came in here about to shout for joy. Well, don't let me spoil it for you. But I'll tell you this, you've made a mistake. I hope it don't turn out tragic for you. And it will if he dies."

Dale Buckley bit his lip slightly, then spoke to me. "Suppose you tell me what happened?"

I did, using very few words. And when I finished, he shook his head. "A damned pity we couldn't have got the hidden assailant in the mine shaft. Of course Jim must have planted him there earlier to get you when you showed yourself." He glanced at Mrs. Dance. "I regret having to speak this way, madam, but circumstances and evidence—"

"Circumstances and evidence, my foot. You've made a mistake."

Dale Buckley sighed; he certainly was a poised man, every bit in control of the situation. "I respect you for feeling that way, Mrs. Dance. Perhaps Wind-River Page

121

could escort you home."

"I'm staying until I know how he is," she said. "Talk all you want. It don't change the truth in my mind."

Buckley glanced at me. "Perhaps we should postpone this to another time."

The door opened and Doctor DuJoir came out, rolling down his sleeves. He lit a cigar before speaking. "I think he'll live. He's as strong as a horse. Of course he'll be flat on his back for a month, but he'll come around." He looked at Mrs. Dance. "You're the marshal's mother? Cry if you want."

"My tears dried up years ago," she said. "Can I see him?"

"In a moment," the doctor said. "Oddly enough, he wants to see you, young man." He turned and opened the door. "I'll give you five minutes. And not a second more."

"I'll go with you," Buckley said and we stepped into the room.

Jim Bell lay like a pale ghost between white sheets, and when he heard us he opened his eyes. He was still a bit groggy from the pain killer, but he had a strong mind and a desire to speak.

"I figured it out," he said slowly. "You wrote the note?"

I nodded my head and Jim Bell smiled.

"Hell, I thought I was onto something real big."

Dale Buckley said, "What's that supposed to mean, Jim? You know damned well you went there to kill the man who wrote the note just to keep him quiet."

"No, I wanted to arrest him, and sweat what he knew out of him."

"That's a thin story," Buckley said. "I'm sorry I can't buy it, Jim." He sighed and stuck his hands in his pockets. "Jim, you're under arrest. There's no other way. We'll have to get a new city marshal appointed."

"Bill Hickok had it once," I said. "Maybe he'd—"

"No," Bell said flatly. "Buckley, you've got influence. Page can handle it. He's my choice."

Dale Buckley didn't laugh at the idea, but he smiled. "He's a little young to—"

"His age won't matter. Dale, if you never do anything for me, do this."

"Well, I guess it can't hurt to give it a sixty day trial. I don't expect we'll have any more bandit trouble."

The doctor stuck his head in the door. "All right, time's up."

We filed out and Mrs. Dance hurried in. Buckley said, "Page, come on over to the house. We'll talk about it."

"What about me?" grandpa said.

"I guess you'd better go on home, grandpa," I said.

He snorted through his nose. "That's right, go on home, grandpa When I ain't needed, I'm supposed to get on home. All right, I'm goin'!" He glared at both of us and stomped out.

"He's a touchy old coot," Buckley said. "How can you stand him around?" He didn't wait for an answer, but swung down the street, and he didn't say anything until we got into his house. We went into the kitchen and he started to poke up the fire to make some coffee.

Emma heard us and came down the stairs, a heavy robe wrapped about her. I said, "It seems that we're always getting you out of bed."

"I don't mind. Why don't you go into the parlor? I'll bring the coffee in."

Neither of us would argue that; we went in and settled down. Dale Buckley said, "God, he sounded convincing there, didn't he?"

123

"Yes. So does his mother."

Buckley shook his head. "Maternal loyalty, pure and simple. Page, I believe we've broken the back of the bandit gang. Without the information pertaining to gold shipments, they're helpless. From now on it should be a systematic roundup of all who were in on it."

I nodded in agreement. "There's Charles Blake, Clyde Henry, Teel Reno, and the five men who run around with him. Like as not we'll cook Blake's goose good when we find out which smelter he's been taking the stolen gold to. As for rounding up the Henry boys, Mort will talk and I think Clyde will. That'll be enough to swear out a warrant for Teel Reno and his bunch."

"That's something I want to discuss with you," Buckley said. "I think Jim Bell's rather talking through his hat when he wanted you to be appointed marshal. Nothing against you, Page. God knows I think most highly of you, as a man and a friend. But I think it's Hickok's job right down the line. My motives, I admit, are selfish. You work for the stage company, and I'd like to keep you on. Naturally there won't be much shotgun guarding now, but I can use a trouble shooter. There's always something a little haywire with a company or it's operation. Now we're faced with the business of cleaning up the rest of the bandit gang. I want this to be a company bit of business. The time to bring in the marshal will be when we herd them into town and turn them over to him for locking up. Don't you agree?"

"It seems that I couldn't have much authority that way."

"Nonsense. I'll make you a special agent and buy you a badge." He smiled. "And as Jim Bell says, I have enough influence to make the city marshal recognize that authority. How does that sound to you?"

Emma came in with a tray. "It sounds as though you're asking him to give up one dangerous job to accept another."

"Now, dear, why don't you just pour the coffee? Well, Page, what do you say?"

"I say, fine, if you can swing it with the judge. I'd like some legal backing of the badge, if it's all the same to you."

"You'll have exactly that," Buckley said, then leaned back with his coffee cup. "Page, it's been a bad night for all of us. I know how hard it must have been to turn against Jim Bell. But the man made his own bed of thorns, you didn't make it for him. By the way, when's your father coming back?"

"In a couple days, I guess." Then I laughed. "Charles Blake's going to be damned surprised when Teel Reno and his bunch take that shipment to the smelter."

Buckley stared at me. "What shipment? What are you talking about?"

"Grandpa and I scouted out Blake's place the other morning, and we overheard him talking to Mort Henry. He told Mort that there was some stolen gold to be taken to the smelter, so we rummaged around in his mine shaft and found it. Grandpa and I emptied the sacks, refilled them with dirt and took the gold back here. Dad has it, and Rudy, our assayer, says it came from our mine."

"Why wasn't I told about this?"

I shrugged. "I guess dad thought it could wait. It never occurred to me to say anything."

Dale Buckley frowned. "My company insured that gold. A full report of this will have to be made as soon as your father gets back. And in the future, I'd like a little more cooperation."

He reached for the coffee pot and refilled his cup. He smiled at his sister. "I'm sorry we woke you, Emma. It was thoughtless of us."

"It's all right," she said. "I don't see much of Page, so I wouldn't want to miss a chance."

"Now that's real flattery," I said. "If I can ever work myself in a position where I can plan a few days ahead, I'd like to ask you to a dance on Saturday night."

"And I'd like to go, if you can plan ahead."

"I think that was a dig," Dale said, smiling.

"I know; I'm bleeding."

"Seriously," Buckley said, "I'd not plan on much social life until this affair is cleaned up. And I feel confident that there'll be a good sized bonus in it from the company. I'll work very closely with you from now on, and we'll plan carefully every move we make. To begin with, I suggest you get a fast horse from the stable and ride to Belle Fourche. I do believe you said your father was there."

"No, he went to Custer first, then if he turned up nothing, on to Belle Fourche."

"Well, that gives you a fifty-fifty chance of guessing right," Buckley said. "At least you'll arrive about the time your father gets there. If the gold is shipped there, you'll be waiting for Teel Reno and his friends. If not, you can cut south and meet them on the Deadwood road."

"Do you think it's better to take them there?"

"Absolutely," he said. "Page, I'll see the judge in the morning, and by the time you get back, your warrants will be ready, and all the papers signed to make you a special agent."

I grinned and scratched my ear. "Just a minute now. Teel Reno won't be alone. But I will be. And he won't stand still to be arrested."

"I've thought of that," Buckley said. "Stop by on your way out of town and I'll have a letter for you. Present that to the town marshal and you'll have all the help you need." He rubbed his hands together. "Page, you don't know how I've looked forward to this day. The company has been on my back for a long time to clean up this mess. Frankly, if we hadn't done it, they'd have sent out a team of investigators. Of course they wouldn't have turned up anything, but it would have cost me my job."

"No job for you means no job for me," I said and got up. "Dale, do me a favor and keep an eye on Jim Bell."

"He'll be guarded day and night; don't worry."

"That wasn't what I meant."

"Oh," Buckley said. "Sure, Page. If it makes you feel any better."

"It does," I said. "Dale, just after I shot him he told me he wouldn't have shot at me, but at the ambusher in the tunnel."

"That's hard to believe, Page. Bell's smart, and even with buckshot in him, he can think on his feet. You go ahead and do your job. We'll let a jury decide Bell's fate."

CHAPTER 12

WITH DALE BUCKLEY'S LETTER IN MY POCKET, I LEFT Deadwood, making only one stop, my house to tell grandpa where I was going. He put up a fuss because he wasn't included, so I told him to get dressed and to take my horse from the barn behind the house. While he was getting ready, I wrote a note for mother and left it on the kitchen table, under the sugar bowl.

I joined grandpa out back and we left town, taking the stage road for a few miles before cutting across country; I meant to make the best possible time to Belle Fourche, and with grandpa picking the best trails, I didn't see how I could miss.

Dawn found us on a hogback and grandpa dismounted. "Time for my backfat and beans," he said and began to put a fire together. He built it small, Indian style. He fried the backfat in a small skillet, then cooked the beans in the grease, washed the pan with dirt and made coffee, which tasted like mud because grandpa wasn't too meticulous about some things.

"The secret of livin'," grandpa said, as he mounted, "is good food. The way your ma cooks, it's a wonder you're alive."

"I noticed you clean your plate."

"Son, I don't want to hurt her feelings, that's all."

He turned silent so I knew we were in for some traveling. We stopped in Spearfish, which wasn't much of a town at all, just long enough for me to ask the agent whether or not the stage had gone through. It had, barely an hour before, and from the agent's description of the passengers, my father was on it.

We left town in a welter of dust, and three hours later we caught the stage at the summit; the driver was giving the horses a breather after the long pull. I showed him my pass, tied both the horses on behind and got into the coach.

There were two other passengers and we sat down. Father said, "How did it go the other night?"

"He showed up," I said. "He's at Doc DuJoir's place."

"I guess that wraps that up," father said. "Nothing in

128

Custer."

"So I guessed." The other two passengers were listening; they could do nothing else in the crowded coach, but they stared straight ahead to let us know this wasn't any of their business.

Father said, "You two got business in Belle Fourche?"

"We're going to meet some men there," I told him. "Dale thinks they'll show up, since there's nothing doing in Custer."

The driver lurched the coach into motion and I wrapped my arm over the window sill to keep from being jounced about. Father said, "That ought to be a surprise. Pretty well wraps it up, doesn't it?"

"More or less," I said.

Father opened his coat and I saw that he was carrying his cavalry pistol in a shoulder holster. "We'll all meet them," he said, then stared out the window.

When we dismounted in Belle Fourche, it was midafternoon, and the street was quiet; there wasn't much doing in the town, except the smelter; mainly it was going back to ranching country, which seems to be a lot steadier than mining.

We stood on the boardwalk a few minutes, then father saw the marshal's office down the street and went there. We followed him. Homer Breen was the law in town; he was a sallow-faced man with a dry, inscrutable manner, and he examined the court order carefully before handing it back to father.

"Seems to be in order. I'm sure Brady will cooperate with you. His office is at the end of the street. All the ore is brought in there, assayed, and paid for. No one except company men are allowed at the smelter." He glanced at grandpa and me. "What's your business?"

"We're with him," I said. "I'm a special agent with the stage company. Have you seen Teel Reno or any of his men?"

"Not for several months," Breen said. "Why?"

"I'm going to arrest them and take them back to Deadwood for trial."

Homer Breen shrugged. "It's all right with me, but can you handle it alone?"

"If we have to," I said. "Marshal, we could use your help."

"Got warrants?"

I shook my head. "There wasn't time. But they're waiting in Deadwood."

"Then I'd just be taking your word, wouldn't I?"

"It's good," grandpa said flatly.

"Sure, but I don't know any of you at all."

I took the letter from my jacket pocket and handed it to him. "This is my authorization."

He read it, then smiled, "I know Mr. Buckley; he's been here a few times checking on the agent. All right, I can give you a deputy and myself." He folded the letter and put it in his pocket. "I'll have to keep this for the record, in case there's any questions asked."

"If that's my authorization, I ought to have it back," I said. "Hell, I haven't even read it."

"Just states the reason for you being here," Breen said, and got up from behind his desk. "You'll find me on the street most any time today, should Teel show up."

"Thank you," father said and we went out to the walk. "I'm going to Brady's office. Come along if you want."

"I'll walk about a bit," grandpa said and sauntered off down the street.

We found Brady in, and he shook hands all around.

He was a slightly built Irishman with a bulldog cast to his jaw. When father showed him the court order, Brady got out the books.

"I can tell you right off that Blake's got a producing vein there. I guess I've handled over a hundred thousand dollars worth of ore in the last seven months. You can check the exact figures yourself."

Father did, most carefully, then he closed the book. "Mr. Brady, would it surprise you to know that every nickel's worth of gold you've smelted down for him belonged to someone else?"

"Stolen?" Brady's jaw dropped. "We do a lot of work for some of the independents around Deadwood, but there's no way for us to tell whether the gold came from a mine other than the owner who brings it in."

"Well I can tell you," father said and whipped out a bunch of Rudy's assay reports. "Get out your own book and see if these assays don't tally with the ones you ran on Blake's gold. Mineral and impurity content should tally to the letter."

Brady dug out some other books and compared the reports, then he slapped his hand on the desk top. "Mr. Sheridan, we had no idea. We're an honest firm!"

"I'm not blaming you," father said. "But we expect Teel Reno to come in with another shipment. Only this time he'll have sacks of dirt. Stall him. Tell him the assayer's out and to go get a drink; you'll send the report to him. We'll be near at hand when he gets it. And I'd duck out of sight right away because we expect some lead to fly about."

"You can rely on me," Brady said. "By God, I've a notion to get my pistol and join you. We're an honest firm!"

"It's not your fight," father said. "Just see that Teel

131

gets the report. We'll take care of the rest."

We shook hands again and walked down the street to the hotel. Grandpa was standing nearby, examining a horse; he joined us on the porch. Father said, "I think we might as well get a room and wait. We can sleep in pairs with one man on watch."

Without waiting for a comment, he went in and registered, and we followed him up the stairs. The room was typical of hotels, a bit stuffy, with a brass bedstead and a lumpy mattress. Father sat down and took off his shoes, then snapped the pistol free of the spring holster and placed it on the night table. It seemed strange to see him armed, and he handled the weapon with a casual familiarity that I couldn't associate with him.

"Wake me in two hours," he said and stretched out to sleep.

Grandpa sat next to the window, looking out. I took the other pillow off the bed and laid down on the floor. Grandpa said, "What's Teel Reno look like?"

"A long drink of water. Dark hair."

Grandpa just grunted and chewed on his tobacco. I felt asleep, and only when he touched me did I wake up.

"Four men coming into town. Two pack horses. Take a look."

I rubbed my eyes and looked out. "That's Reno." I reached out to shake my father but he had heard us and was already sitting up.

"See anything of Homer Breen?"

"Standin' in the saloon door," grandpa said.

Teel Reno waved at Marshal Breen, then pulled up in front of the saloon and they talked for a few minutes before riding on down to Brady's office.

Father said, "I'd like to know what they talked about. Most friendly conversation." He picked up his pistol and put on his shoes. "Let's go down and wait in the lobby."

Just as we reached the bottom of the stairs, Homer Breen came in. He said, "Saw you go into the hotel. Reno's in town."

"Is that a fact?" father said. "We were sleeping."

"He went on down to Brady's place. How do you want to work this?"

"Don't move until we do. Cover the alley behind the saloon."

"Why there?"

"You asked me how I wanted to work this, didn't you?"

"All right," Breen said. "If they try to get out that way, I'll see that they don't."

He turned and went back across the street and father watched him. "Somehow or another," he said softly, "I don't trust him. Maybe it's because Bell was bad, I don't know. Grandpa, go on over there and buy yourself some beer. I want you on the inside and primed when we walk in."

"A couple of beers ought to prime me," grandpa said, and walked on across the street.

"Page, I'll go in first and move to the left of the door. You move to the right. I can't say which side the bar will be on, but if it's on your side, move until you're standing at the end. That'll give you a clear view all the way down, and of the bartender. If it's on my side, I'll do the same."

"All right."

"We've got to figure that Teel will fight. He knows both of us on sight and he knows who we work for. He won't hesitate an instant, and I don't want you to."

"I figured that."

133

Father sighed and lit a cigar with a steady hand. "We'll wait, but I don't think for long."

Ten minutes later Teel Reno and his men came back to the saloon and went inside. Father took out his watch and looked at it. He looked toward Brady's office and then he saw the man come out and head for the saloon.

I broke open my sawed-off and took out the buckshot loads, replacing them with solid ball in case I had to shoot through an oak table top. And at the range this trouble was going to pop, I didn't need a load that scattered.

"That's a fearful looking weapon," father said, and it struck me that he was right. The barrels were only ten inches long, and big enough to stick your index finger into. There was no stock at all, just a rounded butt where the pistol grip ended.

"Let's go," father said and we wasted no time crossing the street. As we reached the bat-wing doors, I heard Teel Reno roar in anger, then we pushed in and I moved into position. The bar was on my side, and before Teel even knew what was happening, I was standing there, the sawed-off resting on the polished mahogany, in clear view of all. Three local men were there, sipping beer, and they moved away fast. Father stood with his hand under his coat; I could see him out of the tail of my eye, and grandpa sat at one of the tables, his long rifle casually laid across it, but pointing at their collective backs.

"Reno, you're under arrest," I said. Then I pointed to the men with him. "That includes you. Don't make any move to resist."

He looked at me, then swung his head and looked at father. "What kind of a deal is this, Sheridan?"

"A lawful arrest," father said. "Look at the odds, Teel.

134

You'll never fight your way out of this one."

Teel Reno considered them, then said, "It's fight now or get hung by a jury. Ray, Curley, you take the kid. Sandy, you and I can outdraw his old man."

Grandpa spoke up. "Do one of you think you can whirl around in time to beat me?"

Teel Reno stiffened, and the one called Curley said, "Teel, there's two barrels to that shotgun."

"So? You want to live forever?"

"No, just a bit longer."

The bartender licked his lips. "Gentlemen, do you mind if I remove myself from the line of fire?"

"Stay where you are," Teel Reno ordered.

I said, "Move back."

"Move," Reno said, "and you'll start the ball. That's a promise."

"Go ahead and move," father said. "If he wants to start it then, we'll finish it."

Sandy, who stood next to Reno said, "God damn it, Teel, can't you see that they've got us braced?"

"It looks like a stand-off to me," Reno said flatly. "I can get Sheridan anyway. And one of you can get the kid."

"Yeah," Ray said nervously. "While we catch a buffalo slug in the back and buckshot from the front."

"There's solid ball in both barrels," I said calmly, "if that makes you feel any better."

"Jesus," Curley said softly. "I can't buck that, Teel. Use your head."

"Head, or gun hand," father said. "Make up your mind and be quick about it." He took out his watch and held it in his palm. "I'll give you fifteen seconds to start shooting or put your hands back on the bar."

The bartender, who had been rooted there, moved

135

back out of harm's way, and there wasn't a sound in the room save the ticking of father's watch, which seemed very loud to me. Teel Reno played it to the wire, then he sighed and put his hands on the bar and the others followed his example. He stood with his head down while grandpa came up behind them and took their guns.

A whistle brought Marshal Homer Breen into the room from the alley. He grinned and said, "You gents want deputies' jobs?"

Teel Reno looked at him. "Some friend. You could have warned me."

"What did I ever owe you, anyway?" Breen asked and produced handcuffs.

Father took his hand away from the butt of his pistol and ordered a glass of beer.

CHAPTER 13

As soon as we returned to Deadwood with the prisoners, I could see that word had gone on ahead, and the fact that we had taken Teel Reno and his friends without firing a shot unpressed everyone.

Particularly Dale Buckley. We were closeted in his office and he was busy making final plans to capture the two surviving Henry boys and Charles Blake.

"As I see it, Blake was the contact man, but the details are a little obscure as to what signal arrangement he had between himself and Jim Bell. I think we need to be in possession of a few more facts before we move against Blake." He glanced at me. "Page, I want you to see Jim Bell, talk to him, convince him that he should cooperate. You can assure him that I'll do everything in my power to get his sentence reduced if he cooperates."

"Reduced from what, Dale?"

"Likely they'll hang him. I'll see that it's a stretch in prison." He looked at his watch. "Suppose you come back in two hours. And be persuasive."

"I'll try," I said and left the office.

I climbed the stairs to Doctor DuJoir's place and found a stage company man sitting there, with a pistol stuck in his belt. From the way he had his chair tipped back against the wall, I knew he'd been guarding the door for some time.

"Is Doc DuJoir in?"

"Out," the man said. "But Bell's in. I see to that."

"Big job," I said and went on in. Jim was still in the back bedroom and when I opened the door, he looked around.

"You put six pieces of buckshot in me," Jim Bell said.

"I'm sorry about that, but you made me do it." I sat down in a chair near his bed. "Jim, give me the straight of it now. I don't want any kind of a lie."

"Page, I've never lied to you." He sighed. "Damn it, I wish you'd believe me. Or just suppose for ten minutes that I'm telling the truth. Can you go along with that?"

"All right."

"You've got to start off believing I'm not the right man. I never gave out information to the bandits."

"You worked with Blake. You told me that yourself. And he's in as deep as a man can get."

"Blake came to me," Bell said. "He told me he'd been approached by the bandits, who wanted to work out of his mine. Blake swore that he had a reputation to protect, and that he was alone and being threatened. He felt that he had to go along with them, but he wanted to

137

cooperate with the law. What could I do but say yes? It was a lead, a straw to grasp at when there hadn't been any straws at all."

"What kind of information did Blake ever give you?"

"Very little," Bell admitted. "But I couldn't press the man. He had to work at his own pace; I could understand that. Anyway, Dale hired you and then things started hopping. It wasn't easy to hold up a stage, and the pressure started getting too much to stand. I was sorry for you, Page, but it gave me hope that I was going to get a break, make a good arrest, something that would stick in Judge Wayne's court." He shook his head. "But it didn't work out that way."

"Sure, because you blocked me every step of the way," I said.

Bell exhibited an impatience with me. "Page, damn it, you never let me in on what you were doing! Never mind that now. Then I got the note, and I thought, here's my chance to grab someone who can talk, who knows what's going on. It turned out to be you, another damned fizzle."

"That's pretty thin, Jim, figuring that you had a man in the mine waiting to bushwhack me."

"Not my man," Bell said flatly. "Page, I came alone."

"And when you reached for your gun, you were going to turn it on the fella in the mine and not me?"

"That's right. Believe that or not, but it's the truth."

I got up and turned to the window and stood there, looking into the alley. "It just doesn't add up in your favor, Jim. It's just your word, your story. We're going to capture Charles Blake and make him talk." I turned and looked at him. "Suppose he tells us that you're the brains behind it all, the man passing on information?"

"He might be saying that, I guess," Bell said. "But he'd be lying, and you'd know it."

"How?"

"Because he wouldn't know I was supposed to signal him." He pointed to his coat. "Page, light me a cigar. They're in the breast pocket. No, I've been doing some thinking while I've been cooped up here. The signal had to be given after the stage pulled into town and parked in front of the office. And there would never be much time, either. And the signal couldn't be more than a subtle movement of the hand or something like that, something so common no one would notice unless he was looking for it and knew it to be a signal."

I handed him his cigar. "A signal you could make as well as anyone else, Jim." I took my seat again. "Jim, face the facts. Buckley is beyond question. His reaction to my note was one of outrage. My father reacted the same way. Dale hired mc to protect the gold, and has helped me in every way to do in the bandit gang. My father helped capture the Reno bunch in Belle Fourche. No, Jim, it's all left you pretty much out on a limb. Surely you see that."

"Yes," he said, "but damn it, I can't give up, just because the odds are against me." He puffed for a time on his cigar. "I haven't convinced you, have I?"

I shook my head. "Dale's offering you a deal, Jim. If you tell him how the whole thing worked, he'll do his best to get your sentence lightened."

"Tell him what? What I don't know?" He slapped his hand against the covers. "Page, will you do something for me? A personal favor?"

"Sure, Jim."

"No matter what the jury decides, keep this thought in mind: that the wrong man has been hung before. Keep it

139

in mind and go on looking and you're bound to discover that I wasn't guilty."

His voice was so steady, so full of conviction that I couldn't refuse him. "All right, I'll do that. But who do I suspect? My father? Dale Buckley? They're the only two left, Jim."

"Suspect a smart man, Page. A man so smart that he's completely outguessed you at every turn of the road. Outguessed me too. He's the man who's beyond suspicion, Page. The last man in the world you'd think about."

"It still boils down to dad and Dale Buckley."

"You made a promise," Bell reminded me. "I'll hold you to it from the grave, Page."

"That doesn't make me feel too good, you talking like that. It makes me feel like I put you there."

"Well, if you'd have shot six inches to the right, I'd be there," Bell said. "And, Page, you look after ma, huh?"

"You want me to drop around and see her?"

"I wish you would."

"All right," I said and went out.

The last person I expected to find at Mrs. Dance's house was Emma Buckley; she answered the door when I knocked and took me into the parlor. Mrs. Dance was sewing; I suppose she needed something to keep her mind occupied.

She looked up when Emma brought me into the room, then said, "Sit down, young man." I looked around, then sat down on the sofa by Emma "I rather hoped you'd come around," she said. "Emma, get the things out of the desk that I showed you."

"Mrs. Dance'" I said, "you don't have to—"

"I do things in my own way," she said. Then she

140

took the small metal box Emma handed her. "This is a bank book," she said. "And here are the deposit slips, still in the envelopes; you can check the postal clerk's mark and the dates on the slips. They date back seven years, and they total up to nearly four thousand dollars, my son's savings in a Denver bank." She handed them to me. "Does that look like the bank account of a bandit?"

I didn't bother to examine the bank book. "Mrs. Dance, these don't really prove a thing, one way or another."

"To a court of law, perhaps not. But to a mother's heart, they prove enough, if I ever needed proof." She leaned toward me. "Young man, I raised that boy, taught him, and I know what kind of a man he is. A mountain of proof to the contrary would not make me believe it."

"Page," Emma said, "don't stop looking now. That's all I'm asking."

I turned and looked at her. "Who's left besides your brother and my father?"

"My brother's not guilty!" she said.

"I see. It's my father then?"

"It's one of the three," Mrs. Dance said softly. "And no matter who it is, someone we all like very much is going to be hurt. No matter who, we've got to hurt one another. There's no way out of it." She shook her head. "If it's my son, I'm hurt, and you too, Page, because your hand brought him down. We've become entangled, we three, and there's no separating us now."

"I'm going over the jail to talk to Teel Reno," I said. "He ought to be able to throw some light on the subject, one way or another. And I guess Dale and I and dad are going to Blake's place to arrest him and the two Henry boys." I got up. "Mrs. Dance, if I learn anything, good or bad, I'll tell you."

Emma went with me to the door and we stood there for a moment, talking softly. "Page, it's sad, isn't it? Faith isn't easy, and to have something gnawing at it—"

"She hasn't seen him for some years," I said. "A man can change, Emma. For good or bad." I put my hand to her cheek and she didn't pull away, so I obeyed a strong impulse and kissed her. "I like you, Emma."

Then my nerve left me and I hurried on down the path before I really did something foolish. A special marshal was sitting in Bell's office, his feet cocked up on the desk. He looked a bit displeased because I interrupted his peace.

"I want to talk to Teel Reno."

He took his feet off the desk. "Leave your gun here."

"I'm not armed," I said and followed him to the cell block. He unlocked the door, let me in, and locked it behind me. Reno was on the bunk and he got up.

"Well, well," he said. "I thought I'd see you again." He hitched up his suspenders. "When I get out of here—"

"You're not getting out," I said. "Reno, how would you like to make a deal?"

"What kind of a deal?"

"Something that might get you ten years instead of a neck stretching."

He regarded me solemnly. "Can you make that kind of a deal?"

"My boss can. Sit down. Let's talk about it."

The cell Reno occupied was separated from the others only by bars running from floor to ceiling, and anything I said to the man could be heard by his friends; they crowded against the bars to listen, which was what I wanted.

Reno said, "What do I talk about?"

"About your life as a bandit," I said.

"I never held up a stage in my life," Reno said.

"But you know who did."

"Sure, the Henry boys. They were the stick-up men."

I turned and looked at Curley and the others. "Today I'm buying information. You're in trouble, so why bargain? I want the facts about this operation. Who's the boss?"

"Doc Blake," Curley said. "There isn't anyone else."

"How does he get his information as to when a stage is carrying gold?"

Curley shrugged. "I don't know. Reno, do you know?"

Teel Reno shook his head. "He just has it, that's all. The only time he was wrong was the other night. Deke Henry was told there was gold aboard, but I hear it was just sand."

"How did you get started with Blake, Teel?"

He looked at me and laughed, then sat down on his bunk. "I went broke in a game. Blake told me he could fix me up with a new stake."

"When was this?"

"Before the robbers ever started working. Blake would get the information, pass it on to the Henry boys, and they'd lift the gold out on the road. We'd be waiting nearby, and take it to Blake's place while they scooted on back to town. That way, if there was ever a slip, they wouldn't have it on them. Then later, when there was time, we'd take the stuff into Belle Fourche to the smelter. Blake had a mine, so there wasn't any reason for Brady to think it hadn't come from his shaft."

"Who killed that other guard Buckley had hired?"

"Deke Henry," Curley said.

"I suppose all of you would swear to this on the witness stand?"

"Hell yes," Teel Reno said. "It's the truth. Look, I'll do time in the pen, but to hang for robbing the stages is something else again. Blake paid us good, but not that good. Besides, he's always said that he only got a fifty-percent cut anyway. The rest went to the contact man, in cash." He laughed. "It's funny, because Blake's been trying to think of a way to get rid of him for a long time, but there isn't any way. Without him, every stage that left town would have to be stopped, and sonny, you've showed the Henry boys how unhealthy that can be." He squinted at me in frank curiosity. "By rights, you ought to be dead by now. Deke and his brothers tried hard enough, I guess, but they've been having a streak of bad luck."

"Yes," I said, "and it's going to get worse." I rattled the door so the marshal would come and let me out. Then I tried a parting shot "Well, it looks like the profit is gone. We've got Bell and you and by tonight we'll have Blake and the two Henry boys."

"Bell?" Teel Reno said. Then he laughed. "What's he supposed to be?"

"The man who really set this up," I said.

Reno looked at his friends, and they all laughed heartily.

"What's so damned funny?" I asked.

Teel Reno said, "Kid, the first stage was stopped a year ago in August. Bell wasn't even in town then."

"He's been marshal here for—"

"I know how long he's been here," Reno said flatly. "But Bell had just had a shoot out with the Jenner twins out at the old Double Deuce mine. Don't you remember? He went to Minneapolis for three months while his leg healed up. That was before the first stage holdup, and he didn't come back until after the fourth robbery."

The whole thing came back to me like a nudge in the back; of course Bell had been gone. The gunfight with Ike and Nate Jenner had been the talk of the town for months; Bell had faced them both down, taken a bad rifle wound in the leg, but had killed both of them.

"Reno," I said, "I really want to thank you."

"Did I do somethin' good?"

"Probably for the first time in your life," I said and went out. A whirl of possibilities came to me in a rush. With Bell gone, he couldn't have set this up, and if he had, he sure couldn't have given out the information on shipments. He'd been telling me the truth, which made me feel fine. But it also made me feel miserable for it pointed the finger at two other men, my own father and Dale Buckley.

CHAPTER 14

THERE WASN'T MUCH DOUBT IN MY MIND AS TO WHAT I had to do, so I went back to Doctor DuJoir's place, only this time I took along a present for Jim Bell.

The guard was asleep and got sore because I woke him, but I told him that it could have been Buckley instead of me, then he'd be looking for another job. He thought that was a good point and sat straighter in his chair as I went inside. The doctor was still out, which suited me fine.

Bell was awake; he seemed puzzled that I'd be back so soon. And his eyes widened in surprise when I took from beneath my coat his pistol and belt. I laid this on the bed by his hand.

"I don't understand," he said.

"Teel Reno convinced me," I said.

"That no-good couldn't convince anyone of anything," Bell said.

"You'd better thank Reno," I told him. "He reminded me that last year, when the robbers started in business, you were in a Minneapolis hospital getting a broken leg fixed." I spread my hands. "Who gave them the first information?"

"By God," Bell said, smiling, "I forgot all about that. That's right! I wasn't even here!"

"Don't get too excited," I reminded him. "I brought your gun because you may need it, and I may need an ace in the hole." Then I got down to business. "We've got two suspects, Jim, and you know without saying which of the two I really suspect."

"Me too," Bell said. "Your dad's been handling millions of dollars a year for as long as I care to recall, and not a cent ever stuck to his fingers. But how can we catch Buckley?" He shook his head. "Oh, it just don't figure at all. He's been doing everything in his power to break up the gang. Could we have missed somebody, Page?"

"It's not impossible that we have," I said. "At any rate, what I know has to stay my secret. You've got to stay here, under guard. You can see that, can't you?"

"Because it might make the real leader careless? Yes, but I don't think he'll be careless. He's too smart for that." He rubbed his face. "Are you going after Blake?"

"Yes, pretty soon now. Dale's organizing it."

"He's probably been warned. Surely after you brought Teel Reno and his bunch back, someone sent word to Blake." He rubbed his cheek again. "If you

146

think about it, send someone around to give me a shave. These whiskers drive a man crazy." He dropped his hand to the quilts. "Page, have you wondered why Blake hasn't turned against Dale, or whoever it is?"

"Yes," I said. "But how can he without cutting himself out? What good does it do to kill the goose who's laying golden eggs? Men like Deke Henry can be replaced. Teel Reno can be replaced. Blake's the kind who sits back and lets someone take the risks for him. Actually, until we get Blake and the man behind him, we haven't broken up the bandit bunch at all."

"You're right there," Ben said. "Damn it, I wish I could get out of this bed."

"Stay put." I got up and turned to the door. "Jim, say nothing of this to your mother. She'd only tell Emma Buckley."

"That's kind of hard on the old girl," Bell said. "All right, Page. Run it your way. But you'll let me know, won't you?"

"Yes," I said and went out.

It was time for me to go to Dale Buckley's office and I found father and grandpa there. Father was carrying a rifle and he was dressed for the rough country. Dale seemed a little put out because I wasn't on time.

"As I was telling your father and Mr. Page, I'm unable to go along with you because of some pressing company business," Dale Buckley said. "Still, I don't think you'll really miss me. Blake, from what I judged in meeting him when he was in jail, doesn't seem like the kind of a man who'd put up much of a fight. And Clyde Henry is in no position to. So you'll just have Mort to worry about."

"We can handle it," father said.

"Of course," Buckley said. He looked at each of us

147

and smiled. "I can't say in words how elated I am that this miserable affair is drawing to a close. My company has lost more than three hundred thousand dollars, all insured, of course."

"And not really lost," I said. "Just transferred to someone else's pocket."

"Lost to me," Buckley said, "and that's all I care about."

"We're wasting time," grandpa said and turned to the door.

The horses were waiting and ready and we mounted up. As we rode out of town, I said, "Blake won't be at his place."

Father looked sharply at me. "Why not?"

"He's been told to get and get fast. And he's already got."

"Then I reckon we'll get after him," grandpa said dryly. "I chased a man for a thousand miles once. Caught him too."

"Who told him to get?" father asked. "Bell's seen no one but you and his mother and Buckley. I haven't been near the man."

"Bell never gave the orders," I said. "Not now or ever."

This brought grandpa's attention around. "You found something out? I told you, didn't I? I told you he wasn't that kind of a man."

"If you know anything, Page—"

"All I know is that he didn't signal anyone. And if you think back, you'll see how I know."

There was a certain amount of pleasure, I discovered, in confounding others, and I fell into a long silence, imitating grandpa. It irritated father and amused grandpa and gave me a sense of maturity, a feeling of equality.

Grandpa set the pace, he wanted to arrive at Blake's place at sundown, or just a bit before. We approached boldly, for in the daylight there was no real blind side to the cabin. I was the first dismounted and I kicked the door open.

Clyde Henry was alone, in bed, and I could see that Blake had amputated the leg. When Henry saw me, he reached for a holstered pistol and I just stepped up to him, swiped his hand away with the barrel of the sawed-off, then threw the pistol into the corner. Clyde Henry was in bad shape.

Father and grandpa came in. Then Clyde Henry said, "He ran off and left me here alone to die."

"Where's your brother?" father asked.

"Gone too."

"We'll have to get him back to town," father said. "Grandpa, go and see if there's a wagon and a team. If there is, fork some hay into the wagon; I'll go back with him."

"Clyde, how much of a start do they have?"

"Four hours, more or less. They left as soon as Blake came back from town."

Father frowned. "Who did he see there?"

"The man," Clyde said. "The man who gives the orders."

"I asked you who?" father said.

Clyde Henry shook his head "I don't know. Blake was the only one, and he would never say. He'd just get the signal, that's all."

"How was he signaled?" I asked. "Clyde, if you know, you'd better tell me. It'll make the difference between a damned rough ride back, or an easy, smooth one."

This wasn't hard for Clyde Henry to decide. He said,

"It was a simple code Blake had worked out. He'd just stand on the street and watch the stage as it made up. Then he'd come back and he'd always know how it was to be." He looked appealingly at each of us. "That's all I know."

"It may be enough," I said Then father and I carried him out, bunk and all, and put him in the wagon load of hay.

Father got on the seat, then said, "Try and take him alive. I want him to speak the man's name."

"You already know his name," I said solemnly.

"Yes, but it will make a better case in court if he's able to speak it." He lashed the team with the reins and drove slowly away.

I was for moving on, but grandpa wanted to look around first, and I thought that he took his own sweet time about it; he spent a half hour in seemingly aimless wandering in circles and sitting down to chew his tobacco. Then he came back.

"They're headin' fer Belle Fourche," he said. Blake's travelin' heavy."

"Carrying gold?"

"Naw. His doctor tools, most likely. The best cover-up a man could have would be a doctor. Some other place he'd just change his name and hang out his sign."

"He won't stop in Belle Fourche," I said. "He's not that stupid."

"But he's goin' there fer a reason," grandpa said. "What could it be, do you suppose?"

"Money," I said quickly. "Blake must have his money in the Belle Fourche bank."

"Good enough," grandpa said, swinging up. "Let's go."

"We'll never catch him."

"We won't try," he said and rode out.

I didn't know what he was going to do, and I knew him well enough not to guess, for I'd be wrong. But when he did it, it was such a fantastic thing that I thought the years had finally caught up with him and that he'd lost his mind. He found the highest rocky prominence in miles and built a fire; then he took the saddle blanket and sent up smoke signals.

Now everyone who lived in the country knew there were Sioux about. We left them alone because we'd had a taste of their war making and didn't want any more of it. Besides, the army kind of looked after them to the extent of drawing their attention away from civilians; they hated the army and got their fill of fighting just tangling with the cavalry.

And here grandpa was, sending smoke signals to attract them.

About ten minutes passed, then grandpa pointed to a blob of rising smoke from a far peak. He whipped his blanket over the fire and spent a furious time holding back smoke, then releasing it. There were answering signals, then he kicked the fire out.

"We wait," he said and bit off a fresh chew of tobacco.

"Now do you mind telling me what that was all about?"

"Had a little talk with the Sioux," he said in his cryptic way. "Used to winter with 'em, long before white men swarmed over these hills and dug holes in it. Oh, I knew there was gold here before Custer found it, but who wanted gold when he had the whole danged sky and a pretty Sioux gal in his blankets?"

"That's a hell of a way to answer a question," I said.

"What answer is there? You don't expect for a minute

151

we could have caught Blake and Mort Henry, do you? As soon as Blake got his hands on that money in Belle Fourche, he'd have gone any direction that came to mind." He settled back and put his hands behind his head. "So I told the Sioux to stop 'em."

"Do you understand smoke talk, grandpa?"

He chuckled. "Boy, all that book readin's fogged your mind. It's only white men with all them words that gets into real trouble. Hell, the Indian's language is simple, only what he needs. There ain't more'n eight words to smoke talk. There's friend, and enemy, and help, and kill, and some numbers, and ways to call friends in to share a good hunt. No, we ain't got a thing to do now but sit here and wait and they'll be brought to us. Sure hope they got enough sense not to put up a fight, because the word's ahead of 'em by now, and they'll be stopped."

"Grandpa, there just ain't no end to you."

He laughed. "Learnin' my way of talk too, ain't you? Stick with me boy, and I'll make a man of you." He raised up to spit tobacco. "Ah, this is good, just bein' out here in the open like this. A man could die here and never have a regret. It's too bad we had to change. A man was better off when he could pick a berry off a bush or kill a bird when he was hungry, and lay down in some cool moss when he got tired."

"A roof's pretty good when it rains, grandpa. Even an Indian's got a tepee."

"True, but a man's got to keep it simple, boy. Women complicate the world. Why, a thousand years ago, a man and his woman lived in caves. I seen some of 'em in Arizona territory. But I know why they ain't livin' there now, why they're all dead and gone. It's because the woman put up a howl for a skin in the cave to make the floor warm, then when she got that, she wanted a pot to cook in, and finally life got so complicated they began to make rules. Which of course leads to fightin' among themselves. Time just killed 'em all off, that's all."

"There are other reasons, grandpa. If you could read, you'd know more."

"Know all I want to know," he said. "Sometimes I think I know too much now."

"I wish you and ma didn't jaw so much," I said.

"Oh, I don't really mind it, I guess," he said. "It's a way to get attention, come to think of it." He watched the sky turn gray and night come on. "We'll have a fire tonight, boy, and hot victuals. Gather up some brush."

It was good, being with him; he was full of adventurous lies and knew how to make the time pass quickly. I've always found it difficult to describe my feelings toward grandpa; I did not want to be like him, not at all. Still I felt privileged that I had known him. He was a hand reaching far into the past, a past my young years denied me, and about him were all those nameless adventures I'd never know. And who knows, perhaps he felt in me a touch of the future, a life that would go on doing long after his own was finished; there was a bond between us, no denying that.

He didn't expect the Indians to show up until morning; the Sioux didn't like to move about at night. He explained the why of their religion to me, but it all seemed pretty silly. Still he spent some time smoothing a spot of earth and making picture writing; it was a message, he said, one they would understand, for since so many years had passed, he expected none to remember him, except in their legends.

I slept the night out without waking, then I heard a horse snort shortly after dawn and sat up. The Indians

153

had come and gone, and they had indeed captured Charles Blake and Mort Henry.

Both men were tied face down on tethered horses.

They were both very dead.

CHAPTER 15

WE TOOK THE TWO DEAD MEN TO DOCTOR DUJOIR'S place, and collected a crowd along the way. Hardly had the bodies been carried inside and decently stretched out when father showed up, and a moment later, Dale Buckley.

He took one look at Charles Blake and said, "It's too bad. We could have used his statement to help convict Jim Bell, but I suppose we'll do all right without it." He took out a handkerchief and wiped his face. "Did you have to kill him?"

"Aren't you happier this way?" father asked.

Buckley looked at him, a puzzled expression on his face. "What do you mean, Fred?"

"You really didn't want him to talk, Dale. He might have said the wrong thing."

"That's ridiculous," Buckley insisted. "I only met the man once in my life, when you had him arrested. Fred, if you're accusing me of anything, you'd better watch yourself."

Father turned to grandpa. "Go get Jim Bell."

"The man's a prisoner!" Buckley snapped. "Fred, you're exceeding your authority!"

"Well don't you worry about it," father said.

Buckley compressed his lips tightly to show his displeasure, then said, "Page, I hope you aren't a party

154

to this nonsense."

"I don't think it's nonsense," I told him and he glared at me.

"Your usefulness to the company has ended," he said. "You're fired."

Grandpa came out of Bell's room, supporting the man, Bell could stand fairly well by himself but he was too weak to move about. Dale Buckley looked at him, and at the gun Bell wore, and he said, "What's the meaning of this? This man is under arrest."

"I un-arrested him before I left town," I said. "He's not the man we want."

"You will find different on the indictment," Buckley said.

"I'll sign the warrant," father said sternly. "Dale, you've made damned few mistakes, I'll admit to that."

"The whole lot of you are insane! You haven't a shred of proof to back you up." He laughed without humor. "Me? Why, I've done everything in my power to break up the gang. Would I hire a shotgun to—"

"You would if you were tired of the whole thing and wanted out," father said. "And they'd be helpless to stop you because they didn't know who the boss was. Blake couldn't act against you without exposing himself; you forced him to go along."

"And I tell you that I don't even know Blake. I challenge you to prove that I do." He waved his fingers under father's nose. "And unless you can prove that, everything you say is a pack of lies."

"I'll tell you how you worked it," father said. "Blake would stand down the street where he could see you come out of the station. The mail pouch was the last thing you brought out. That was the signal for Blake."

Dale Buckley smiled in amusement. "I always carried

155

the pouch out last. If Blake told you that, he lied."

"It was the way you gave the pouch to the driver," father said. "Sometimes you handed it to him, and other times you tossed it to him." He looked steadily at Dale Buckley. "Do you still insist that Blake was lying?"

"Certainly." He looked at grandpa and me. "You two weren't smart, killing them. Whatever Blake said is worthless because he's not here to back it up. And that's too bad, because there was the only proof you have to these outrageous charges." He pointed to Jim Bell, who just stood there, taking it all in. "You're letting a friendship for this man color your judgment. Well, a court will decide the truth."

A woman's step came across the porch, then Emma Buckley burst into the doctor's waiting room. "Page, are you all right?"

"I'm fine," I said and put an arm around her.

Dale Buckley said, "Would one of you have the decency to close that door? I don't want my sister looking at dead men."

She glanced at me, then at Dale, as though she didn't know what he was talking about, then she looked through the door and into DuJoir's operating room.

When she gasped, I took it for a natural reaction. Then she said, "Dale!"

"I'll close the damned door them" he snapped and jerked past me.

But father stiff-armed him and shoved him back, while Emma left the circle of my arms. Dale said, "Emma, it's not for your eyes!"

She didn't seem to hear him at all, or if she did, she chose to ignore him. She went as far as the open doorway and looked at Charles Blake for several minutes, then she whirled on her brother, her expression

156

puzzled. "Frank Rogers here in Deadwood? Dale, you told me you'd broken with him. You lied to me, after you'd promised."

There was a whisper and a metallic click as a hammer went back, then I saw Buckley freeze; he stood under the muzzle of Jim Bell's .45. Bell said, "Suppose you tell us about Blake, Emma."

"Blake? His name is Frank Rogers. He and Dale were way and looked at Charles Blake for several minutes, good. He was kicked out of medical school three years ago. Dale, you promised father that if he'd give you this job you'd have nothing more to do with him."

"So you didn't know each other," father said.

Buckley looked at Emma. "You fool! You headstrong, nosy fool." Then the anger left him and he let his shoulders sag. "All right, I knew Frank."

"And of course this was all his idea," father suggested.

Emma looked at each of us; she didn't say anything, but understanding came to her and her expression cracked like a cold jar with hot water poured into it. Bell said, "Page, get her out of here. Take her to ma."

"But—"

"Don't argue, son," father said.

I put my arm around Emma and led her out of the place and down the street. Mrs. Dance answered the door and when she saw Emma, her face took on a deep sadness. "There's just no getting around the hurt," she said. "Just no getting around it at all."

I wanted to stay, but my place was back there with my father so I turned down the path. The shot wasn't very loud, rather a small, ineffectual pop. Then I heard Bell's .45 roar and saw Dale Buckley plunge off the porch, hit the street rolling, and tear across.

Traffic saved him; neither father nor Bell wanted to fire into it. I started to run toward the stage office; that was where Buckley headed, and my father saw me and shouted something to me, but I couldn't make it out.

Never have I seen the main street clear up that fast; within a minute horsemen and pedestrians had vanished. I ran down the walk like a dumb fool, and Bell yelled, "Take cover, damn it!"

He didn't say that any too soon, for Buckley popped out with his shotgun, flung it up and sent a charge of shot whistling through the spot where I had been. I plastered myself against the saloon wall and wished I had another twenty inches of barrel on my sawed-off; he was way out of my range and he'd kill me before I could get near him.

Dale was shouldering his gun for his second shot and I backed up a step, still plastering myself against the wall. There wasn't much protection, but I knew that if his aim was in the least faulty, he'd bounce the shot off the wall and miss me.

Then the wall gave way and I fell inside the saloon before I realized that I'd backed up and leaned against the swinging doors. I got up and foolishly brushed the sawdust from my clothes and hoped that Dale would be dumb enough to come after me; he'd narrow the range to where I could get in a shot.

Then I thought, to hell with it; I've got to go to him, and wondered what I'd use for cover. When I looked around the room, the crowd backed up a step or two, and it gave me an odd feeling, to know that people were afraid of me, even for an instant.

I picked up one of the oak poker tables; it was nearly four feet across and an inch thick, enough to stop shotgun pellets, and I staggered out with it. I simply rolled it off the porch and into the street and rolled with it, and Dale Buckley put a charge of buckshot into it. He was sixty yards away, on the walk, and I pushed toward him, keeping down, keeping the table before me.

He shouldered the gun, and I yelled at him, "One shot left, Dale! Use it and I'll get you before you can reload!"

It was enough to make him hold his fire; he stood there, the gun to his shoulder, and I brought the range to forty yards. He knew he couldn't get through the oak table top to me, and I wasn't showing any of myself, pushing it along ahead of me and crouching down behind it.

I thought it was time for one last gamble. "I've got both barrels left, Dale. Now if I pop up, can you get me first? Or will I catch you? You know how this thing scatters, and I'll let go both barrels."

Why grandpa or father or Bell didn't cut him down was beyond my understanding, and I held this inaction against them. I moved the table to thirty yards and suddenly flung myself clear of it. He touched off his last shot and; the pellets rattled into the oak, then I stood up while he looked at the gun as though it had betrayed him.

"You were always a lousy wing shot," I said. He threw the shotgun into the dirt. "It's too bad you missed me at the mine."

"I was shooting at Bell," he said solemnly. "Page, I don't want to hang."

"That's not up to me."

Grandpa and father ran toward me; Jim Bell stayed on the doctor's porch.

"Why the hell didn't you shoot?" I asked when they came up.

"I was thinking of the girl," father said. "Weren't you?" He looked at Dale Buckley. "Why did you do it?"

"For money. What else?" He looked at me and smiled sadly. "I wanted out, Page. I wanted to be done with it; I had enough to go somewhere and make a real start. You almost did it my way, but damn you, you had to do a real good job."

They took him to jail and locked him up and father swore out the complaint and Dale Buckley signed a confession. And I felt simply rotten about the whole thing, and nothing Jim Bell or father could say would shake me out of it. Even grandpa couldn't do it.

Still there was work to be done, work I hadn't counted on. The stage maintained a schedule and carried mail, and there wasn't any reason for it not to go through, at least one the government would understand.

A postal inspector arrived a week later, made an investigation, and made me manager of the Deadwood branch; he had a letter of authority from the Board of Directors, and signed by Dale Buckley's father, who was on his way west.

Jim Bell was feeling well enough to walk about a bit; he told me how Buckley had made his break at DuJoir's office. Buckley had been carrying a small .32 single-shot, and he fired it point blank at Jim Bell's stomach, only the thick bandages stopped the bullet.

I made no attempt to see Emma Buckley; I felt that she must hate me for what I'd done, and hate herself a little too for tipping the scales so greatly against her own brother.

Grandpa came in one morning, thirty dollars in hand, and announced that he wanted a ticket for somewhere; he wasn't particular just where. It seems that ma had asked him to paint the barn and he had balked.

I said, "Grandpa, we all got to work for our keep."

"I work at what strikes my fancy," he said. "You goin' to sell me a ticket or ain't you? I'm gittin'."

"That's because you're not man enough to stick it out," I said.

He bristled at me. "Watch your talk there, sonny. I'm Wind-River Page!"

"Probably more like Windy Page, if the truth were known." I got up and came from around the desk. "Grandpa, the day you stopped here, you challenged me to a fight to see what I was made of. All right, you old horse thief, I'll challenge you to one, no holds barred, to see what *you're* made of."

"Boy, I'll whup you proper. No holds style is mountain style, and if you think I wouldn't gouge an eye out or bite an ear off because you're kin, think again."

"Grandpa, you don't scare me a damned bit. You want to step outside or not?"

He let out a ringing whoop of joy, put his sack and rifle down and stepped to the street. I don't know, I guess it's the way men who are about to fight carry themselves; there is some sign that draws other men; we had a circle about us before I could get my coat off.

Grandpa came at me like a panther, as fast and as savage, and he opened a cut above my eye before I could get in a lick. I sank a fist into his stomach and it was like hitting a plank door, but he grunted and we danced away. In my mind I had the notion to go easy, on account of his age, but experience had already taught me to give him all I had and hope it would be enough.

I knocked him flat on his back and watched him bounce erect, his mouth bleeding. We wrestled and kicked and I spent half my time fending off his damned teeth and fingernails, but I was beginning to hurt him, for his breathing came hard and his eyes were turning glassy. I worked on his stomach and under the heart; ma'd fly into a fit if I marked up his face. But a couple times I caught him on the jaw and put him down, and four times I had to get up from the dirt myself; he was a tough old buzzard with a punch like a young mule.

He was slowing down, and so was I, and my head kept ringing and it was now and then difficult to focus my eyes. Then I caught him with his stomach muscles loose and doubled him over. His jaw was sticking way out, unprotected, and it was too good to pass up; I put him flat on his back and this time he didn't get up.

The crowd parted while I dragged him over to the horse trough and dumped him in, then I noticed that my father was standing there, watching me, and I couldn't tell whether he was furious or not.

Grandpa suddenly sputtered and sat up and shook his head, throwing water like a shaking dog. He looked at me, then said, "I been licked, huh?"

"You've been licked," I said.

He started to get out of the trough. "I guess that settles that."

"Nothing's settled," I told him. "We're not through yet."

"We ain't?"

"No, we're going over to the barbershop."

"What for?"

"So you can get a haircut and a shave and a bath."

"I won't do it!"

"You'll do it or take another licking," I said. "Grandpa, it's about time you acted civilized." He was going to get stubborn, so I fisted a handful of soggy

162

collar and hauled him out of the watering trough. "Now you stay here," I said and went inside for his stuff. The sack of clothes I threw into the watering trough, then I swung the rifle against the cast iron hitching post, put a good crimp the barrel, and dropped it in the gutter.

He roared and swung on me and I knocked him back into the water, then hauled him out again. The nearest barbershop was six doors down and I booted him along ahead of me.

Making him take a bath almost took another fist fight, but he gave in to me, then sat in the chair while the barber plied clippers and razor. He submitted, under protest, and the barber wouldn't charge me a dime; he was that glad to get grandpa out of the chair. Then I marched him down to Herb Meadow's Dry Goods store, and using my credit, I decked him out from head to foot with a dark suit, a nice tie and a ruffled shirt. When I told Meadows to take his old clothes and burn them, grandpa set up a howl, but I was firm with him.

"You won't need 'em anymore, grandpa. Can't you see that?"

He nodded. "I can see it, but do I have to like it?"

"You'll like it," I assured him. "You look good, grandpa."

"Hogwash!" He fussed a bit. "I suppose I've got to go home now and parade in front of your ma?" When I didn't answer him, he put on the new hat and said, "Well, let's get it over with. I hate bein' fussed over."

Father had gone on ahead of me; he and mother were waiting on the porch when grandpa and I walked up the path. It was hard to tell about mother; she didn't cry often and when she did I never knew whether it was because she was glad, or sad.

She kissed grandpa's smooth-shaven cheek and said,

"You look nice, papa. Real nice."

Then she held the door open so he could step in. He stopped before the hall mirror and surveyed himself, then he smiled. "I guess I do look pretty good at that."

Father turned to me as though he meant to interrupt, meant to take me aside; he stepped outside with his arm around my shoulders. "Emma Buckley was over this morning. She wants you to come to Mrs. Dance's house for supper." He gave my shoulder a pinch. "I'd go. And wear your good suit."

"Pa, I know what to wear."

"Mmmm," he said. "Grandpa learned late. It strikes me that you're somewhat alike."

"Pa, how old does a man have to be before he gets married?"

He let his eyebrows draw into an irregular line. "Thinking like that, huh?"

"Well, I like Emma a lot."

"Go ahead and like her, son. Fall in love with her if you want, but I don't think you'll marry her. Some other girl, yes. Someone you don't know, or you haven't noticed yet. Page, it takes a woman or two in a man's life to make him aware of women in general. You go ahead with your spooning. Live life, son. It's good." He reached into his pocket and brought out a couple of cigars and offered me one.

"I don't smoke, pa."

"Then it's time you started."

"Ma'll raise hell."

He cleared his throat. "Well, I'll handle her when the time comes. I think." Then he scratched a match and held it for me while I nervously took my first puff.

164